Easter Ann Peters' Operation Cool

JODY LAMB

Easter Ann Peters' Operation Cool

Published by Scribe Publishing Company
Royal Oak, Michigan
www.scribe-publishing.com

Copyright © 2012 by Jody Lamb
Cover illustration © 2012 by Jillian Evelyn

ISBN 978-0-9859562-0-2

Library of Congress Control Number: 2012947114

Printed in the U.S.

DEDICATION

This book is for the extraordinary Brooke Lamb,
my guardian angel in little-sister disguise.

• • • ONE

Okay, seventh grade. Bring it. I'm ready.

Grandma Dottie once told me that sometimes you have to pretend you have a ton of confidence until it's there on its own.

I stand near the parking lot where parents and buses unload kids to wait for the first bell.

This year's going to be a good one. The kind that I need.

Seventh grade's important. Positively. It's the year we officially become teenagers. Coolness at this point can totally wipe out my kindergarten through sixth grade shyness and predictable dorkiness.

I have Operation Cool, my official plan to make seventh grade awesome. It's in a notebook—official and grownup, yet prettified with a purple squiggle under the title on the cover. For good luck, it's stuffed in my backpack between folders. I go over it in my head for the hundredth time:

Step One: Make a good friend. She doesn't have to be a best friend, just a good friend to do stuff with outside of school.

Step Two: Stop clamming up and turning into a statue around boys, especially Tommy Hansen.

Step Three: Have a cool thing I'm known for. Everyone has a thing they're good at, like ballet or basketball or guitar. So far, I'm only good at school. I'll keep getting good grades, but not mark the bar so high that it bugs people.

Step Four: Stand up to Horse Girl, the world's jerkiest seventh grader, known outside of my brain as Erica Morski, the most popular girl at Lake of Eileen Middle School.

It'll work. It's got to. Plus, no more braces will take my coolness level up a notch automatically.

In the parking lot, best friends in clusters laugh over photos on their cell phones. I have one from the Stone Age. No camera. No text. No web. Just a phone, but I'm happy to have that, at least.

The "predator-net," as Dad calls it, is more dangerous for a kid than walking alone at night in a city alley, according to Dad. I'd love to have Internet access on my cell, though. I could keep in touch better with Stephanie, my friend who moved far away two years ago, and my Grandma Dottie.

I tug on my shirt to smooth out the wrinkles. Oh

no! There's a big hole on the side?! You can see my skin through it! Bright pale stands out like the neon Mega Millions sign that hangs in the Lake of Eileen Market window in my town.

It's fine. It's not like I'm raggedy. Just a little hole. On the first day. It's fine! Really!

My whole class is arranged by clique until Horse Girl breaks away from her group, struts up and starts in on me.

"Ha, Easter, where'd you get that shirt?" she asks with her ginormous smile that makes her eyes shrivel to raisins. "Your grandma's closet? Or the Salvation Army, as usual? Or maybe even their dumpster?"

One hour ago, these jeans and this stop-sign red short-sleeve shirt with a drawing of two brightly colored lovebirds together on a tree branch seemed so safe from Horse Girl's snarkiness. That funny-feeling thing makes its way from my stomach, heads up and lands, lump form, in my throat. It's one-hundred percent absolutely worse than the moment before the nurse gives you a shot. Butterflies have a dance party inside of me.

Get a grip.

Heat hits my cheeks at a hundred miles per hour and I don't know what to do but drop my backpack and pretend to look for something in the front pocket. I find nothing but a pink eraser. Great, stupido! Remind them that you're Super Geek! Smart! I stand and thumb the eraser in my hand. Muffled whispers followed by giggles make me stare at the tiles.

Say something!

Horse Girl and her killer sense of humor.

Before my face melts, a girl behind me clears her throat.

"Oh, I really like her outfit," she says.

I twirl on my ballet flats. The girl looks a lot older than me, taller and curvier, with long, smooth, straight brown hair. Totally the kind you see in a shampoo commercial. She has silvery eye shadow, thin pink lips and a zit-free face. What's most shocking is that she's wearing a turquoise sundress with giant white flowers, like the kind I've seen in books about the 1960s. One side is sleeveless and the other has a super poofy, flowy three quarter-length sleeve. It has a round scoop neck and a skinny gold belt. Glamour! In Lake of Eileen!

"In big cities like Chicago, people are into unique clothing," the girl says, like 'I'm right and you know it.'

A circle of people forms around us. The silence roars.

Horse Girl's face is all scrunched up and constipated-ish. She's sizing up the new girl, studying every inch of her. Friend or competition? Typical.

"Everyday store stuff is so…" The girl flicks her nose, like she might be allergic to this place, and leans her body on her right hip. "…boring. A little outside the box is awesome, you know?"

Whoa! What just happened?

Horse Girl's mouth falls a bit and her eyes move half a centimeter per hour from the new girl's shoes up to her face and back down again.

The girl scans the people around, all casual, like what she said was no big deal. It's so un-noisy at this moment, I hear her pencils and pens bumping each other when she looks for something in the side pocket of her purse.

Standing up to a snooty-pants face with snooty pants-ness! That's the kind of thing you appreciate in a person.

But why'd she do that? She's a new girl! Isn't that sort of a rule when you're new, you don't stand up to people? Was she just showing Horse Girl she's not going to be one of her groupies? Like, 'Missy, looky here, I'm an individual.'

We're all statues, standing there, until Horse Girl's face morphs into phony, super-friendly mode and she takes a step closer. "Hiii! Are you new?"

"Yep, just moved here from Chicago," the girl says. "My dad got transferred to an office a ways away from here." She points left, catches herself, shakes her head and points behind her with the other hand that crinkles a blueberry PopTart package. "This place is super tiny compared to where I come from, so this is kind of a big—" She raises arms up, wide like she's holding a hoola hoop in the air "—change for me." She grins, wide enough to show her perfect teeth. "My parents were tired of the crowded city life."

"What's Shacaaago like?" says a kid with a thick Michigan accent like he's never been out of Lake of Eileen.

But Horse Girl's got questions so he'll have to wait. "What grade are you in?" she interrupts.

"Seventh."

"Me too!"

"Oh yeah?" The new girl nods. "I'm Wreni Hammer."

Totally a movie star name.

The circle grows bored and walks away as though nothing has just happened, so Wreni and Horse Girl start walking, too. Horse Girl's always a fast walker, and they pass me right away.

Wreni tears open the PopTart foil and offers Horse Girl half of it. Crumbs settle on the pavement to make a yummy breakfast for some lucky ants. Horse Girl shakes her head and grins.

Great, she just found another member of her adoring crew. They're practically best friends already. There goes that. A chance at Step One shot down before we even walk through the doors.

I'm trailing behind all of the seventh graders when Wreni stops near the door and glances behind her. Her gold sandals clickety clack all the way back to me. Horse Girl glares and stands there watching—long enough to make me nervous about what she's going to do.

"Wow, those are so great," Wreni says and points.

We stare at my flats—black and sprinkled with tiny red roses.

"Oh, thanks." My reply comes out all dry and froggy, which makes her giggle. I do, too.

Come on. Say, 'Hi, I'm Easter.' The words swirl in my head but never make it down to my throat. I stare down at my shoes.

"Mmm hmm," Wreni finally says, maybe to break the awkward moment, and looks away.

The line inches forward and I breathe, but I can't stop wondering about what all of this means. What's the deal with Wreni Hammer, and why would she stick up for me?

Mrs. Martin, our teacher, has gray hair, gray skin, a bottom that weighs down her body, a round face and two chins. She can't pull off a full-fledged walk, but instead shuffles with her bad hip. Today she's wearing a red shirt tucked into a wrinkly black skirt with rulers and red apples all over it.

"Hello, Miss Peters."

Her manly greeting reminds me how on the last day of sixth grade, she came in to meet everyone and said that she was excited to have suuuch a diligent student in her class this year—me. Thanks, Mrs. Martin. Way to start things off for me.

"Hi, Mrs. Martin." I smile a polite one.

"Have a nice summer?" She pats me on the head like I do when I greet my dog Amigo, just to make it absolutely clear that I am her class pet. Great.

Sometimes I think things would be easier if I just decided to become a bad kid.

"Yes, I did, thanks," I say. Please, please don't embarrass me anymore.

Mrs. Martin points behind me. "I don't recognize your face, so you must be Wreni."

"Hi!" Wreni waves and takes two steps forward.

"Well, welcome!"

"Thank you." She mini bows with her head.

The first thing I notice when we make it to the classroom is that Mrs. Martin's skirt is made of the same fabric that covers the bulletin board. Maybe that's super cool in the teacher world.

Rustling stops in the classroom when Wreni enters behind me. We're the last of the seventh graders. It's so quiet, in fact, that I avoid swallowing on account of having a desert-y mouth and not wanting to let out one of those weird nervous swallow sounds.

Everyone scatters to fill the seats, minus the front row, of course. That's reserved for the class pets.

"Class, this is Wreni Hammer." Mrs. Martin motions us to follow her to the front of the room. "She is new. Be niiice." She bugs out her eyes like we're third graders. "She's from the big city with a lot of wind and now she's here in a little town with a big lake!" Mrs. Martin chuckles so hard, her belly shakes. I doubt she'll ever realize her jokes are only hilarious to her. She points to the only remaining non-front row desk way on the other side of the room and asks Wreni to settle there.

Wreni nods and scans the room of eyeballs. "Hi," she says, all casual like she's known us forever. Then she clickety clacks to the chair, smoothes her dress and sits.

She doesn't seem nervous at all!

I'm headed to the front row when Mrs. Martin says, "So that Wreni can get to know us faster, we're all going to introduce ourselves. Easter, since you're standing, how about you go first? Say your name and one interesting thing about you."

Thirty pairs of eyes stare.

"Um, hi." I shoot my right arm up in an awkward salute/wave. "Uh, I'm Easter and…" Think. "Um, one interesting thing about me is, uh, uh, I guess I'd say…"

Horse Girl giggles.

"Well, I have a cat, a dog and a goldfish." Pathetic!

I claim the front row seat that's four rows away from Wreni and two seats ahead of Horse Girl. How could I blank out like that?

My heart sways down to my belly like a feather from a bird's nest to the grass.

Coolness is not going to come easy.

Tommy Hansen volunteers to go next.

He shares seven funny 'I'm awesome-but-I-really-don't-know-it' things about himself. Not that it even matters what he says anyway. Like even 'My doo doo stinks big time,' would be totally amazing, too.

What's most fascinating about Tommy Hansen is the way he instantly draws the attention of everyone in the room like bugs to the lamp outside. Without trying. It's because when you're near him, you feel like you're hanging with a celebrity. He is stunningly movie star handsome, on a Lake of Eileen scale at least. It's the wavy brown hair and how he makes the other guys look so young with his muscle-y arms and the fact that he's high-schooler tall. That also makes him super great at sports. That's his thing.

On his way back to his seat, Tommy picks up a pencil from the floor and holds it out to me.

"Oh um" trips out. For goodness' sake.

"Thanks, that's mine," the kid to my right says and snatches it, but Tommy smirks AT ME. Like he's saying, 'Hi.'

I'm sure of this at first, but then my brain takes over. No, that can't be right. He never even looks at me for longer than a millisecond. Someone behind me is smiling back, I bet. DO NOT TURN AROUND. They'll see me turn, and it'll be all awkward. They'll know I thought he was smiling at me.

After everyone introduces themselves, all relaxed with extraordinarily interesting things to say, Mrs. Martin tells us to chat about summer and stuff with a neighbor while she gets a presentation up and running.

Horse Girl's the loudest, so a third of us hear all about her fabulous summer, complete with oh-so-hilarious imitations of her crazy old-lady neighbor. Of course, she also makes time for stories about the cute high school boy she worked with at her grandpa's hardware store who told her she's "so cute."

And did Horse Girl stuff her bra or did it actually double in size over the summer? Her hair is tousled but pony-tailed up so it's still quite horse-butt like. Her hair has been a blend of blond and brown highlights for so long now no one remembers what color actually grows out of her head. Her eyebrows, which are blondish brown, are thinner and arched now. This actually makes her look more like a horse, at least in my mind. You should see the way she cackles super loud and hyena style, with tall, bright pink gums. No one teases her about it, though. Prettiness + the ability to come up with jokes like no big deal and do imitations that make people laugh until their insides twist = you're the most popular girl in school.

I scoot my chair to rest my elbows on the desk, but my stomach bumps it and it skids a few inches. Thank goodness it's loud in the room; I figure no one hears or bothers to look my way.

"Sorry!" I shift like it's possible to find a comfortable spot on the rock-hard seat.

"Easter."

I can't tell who said my name, so I glance to my left and my right. No one's looking.

I'm losing my mind.

"Hey, Easter." From behind.

I turn and grip my chair.

Connor Cruz's head is tipped.

"Did you just say sorry to your desk?"

"Um." I search for the instant replay, but everything's running together and my head empties. "Did I?"

"Yeah, I think you did."

"Oh, I guess I did."

"Polite!"

"Ha, yeah." I nod and stare at his desk's scratched-up metal feet.

Connor's liked by everyone, but he's pretty much clique-less. He's kinda weird because he's really into movies—he's like a walking history book of films. If you're ever on one of those trivia shows, he'd be the person to call if there's a movie category. He's taller this year—about the same height as me, which is average for a girl but kind of short for a boy in the seventh grade.

"Hello, desk," he whispers, leaning in super close to the top. "I'm Connor. Nice to meet ya." He wipes his hand across the top, rubs the corner twice and squishes up his nose. "You smell bad! Must be booger-killing chemicals."

Someone smiling really big with dimples makes you smile, too, even when it's not totally clear if someone's making fun of you or not. It's a reflex, like when the doctor whacks your knee with a mini hammer.

Say something funny back. I search my brain. Nothing.

Two seconds too many pass, so I hmm-hmm giggle and spin around.

I should have laughed a real laugh! That was the kind of laugh you give out of niceness when an old person tells a knock-knock joke or pulls a quarter from behind your ear.

Lukewarm Lame. That's what I picture myself updating the status of Operation Cool to tonight, thanks to me pulling idiot moves like this.

Day One of the most important year of my life = Not so great.

"Hey, ya!" Wreni appears next to me on the blacktop as we near the buses.

"Oh, hey!" Don't be a dork.

"Easter, right? That's really your name?"

I pause for a sec, wondering if she's going to tease or what. "Yep," I finally say. "That's my name."

"Huh!" She nods, like 'hmmm, interesting' and stares at me like I should have some funny response because I probably get that kind of reaction just about every time I say my name.

I swallow and it's loud.

The kid in front of us glances back with his mouth hanging open, like he's wondering why the cool new girl is talking to me.

So then this flies out of my mouth at a thousand miles per hour: "Oh, well, you probably think I was actually born on Easter Sunday. That would make sense. But I wasn't. My mom was in labor at dawn on Easter morning but I didn't decide to come out until just after midnight, so it was the day after, technically. My parents couldn't agree on a name beyond Easter. They're pretty much opposites. My grandma told them that it was still Easter Sunday on the west coast and that it was a holy-ish name and stuff so they stuck with it." Quit rambling. "So, yeah, that's how I got named."

"Hilarious." She smiles, but I can't tell if it's real-nice or fake-nice, like inside, she might be thinking, 'That's super weird.' But then she says, "I wanna be named after a holiday, too. Like St. Patty or Thanksgiving."

I snicker and she does, too, because she seems totally serious about it.

"This is my bus, so…" I smile an awkward kind. "I guess I'll see ya tomorrow." I turn and walk a yard toward the purring engine part of the bus.

"Bye, Easter!" She mini waves and grins big enough to show her teeth.

I close my eyes and make a wish. Please let her be my best friend. Please times a gazillion. If I can complete Step One right away, Operation Cool might actually work.

• • • TWO

Yoplait, my cat, charges down the stairs and leaps from the bottom step to my feet before the front door is even shut.

"Hey, girl!"

She rubs her head against my leg and fur flies like how the wind scatters dandelion seeds in summer. Her fur is always flying like that because it's long, thick and covered in giant splotches of peach and white. I think it's her super long, puffy tail that'd better fit a Golden Retriever that makes her stand out most.

Against the glass door to the deck, I squint in the sunlight before sliding the door open an inch—still watching Yoplait from the corner of my eye.

"Mom? Home."

She's still in her pajamas. It was a half-day of school so I figure that's okay.

Slower than Mrs. Martin's walk, Mom, on the lounger with a coffee mug, turns to me for half a second. "Okay, hi."

"First day was good! There's a new girl in my class!"

"First day was good?" She takes a big sip and leans back against the lounger.

My zippity-doo-dah enthusiasm deflates. "Yeah, that's what I said. I had a good day."

Silence. I lean on one leg and search for another interesting thing to report about, but I can't think of anything.

"That's nice," she whispers, then closes her eyes. Her slippers fall to the deck floor when she kicks out her feet and crosses her legs.

In the kitchen, Amigo, my old-man mutt, and Yoplait hang out near the cabinet they know stores the treats.

I pinch a mini bone-shaped meat mush and hold it a foot above Amigo's head.

"Amigo, lay down!" I command, grownup-ish.

He sits and raises his right paw up in the air like, 'Hello, nice to meet you.' I don't bother correcting him. His tail wags when he opens his mouth wide, and I toss the treat in.

"Okay, lay down, girl," I tell Yoplait, who's waiting beside Amigo with patience. She plants her butt on the tile, leans forward and lets her front paws slide until she's lying down. Then she rolls over onto her side and stretches her neck to look back at Amigo and make sure he's watching.

"Show off!" I rub her head with one hand. She licks off a tiny triangle of tuna and a half a triangle of chicken from my other hand and trots away with it.

My stomach rumbles to announce it's lunchtime, so I open the cabinet and find that one special little plate with dancing baby chickens all over it. It was my favorite as a little kid. Guess it still is.

I make peanut butter and jelly sandwiches with wheat bread—one for Mom and one for me. I put more peanut butter on hers and more jelly on mine. We have opposite peanut butter and jelly styles.

Like a waitress, I balance two plates on my right arm and carefully slide the door to make an opening big enough for sound to get through but too small for Yoplait's head.

"Ahem, Mother, the chef's finest PB&J awaits you." I say in a fancy butler voice and nod toward the plates.

"Ah, no thanks," she says without looking at me. "I ate a late breakfast."

"You sure?"

"Yeah."

I want to know what she ate because there are no dishes in the sink or dishwasher, but I decide not to ask.

While I'm eating at the counter, Mom, swaddled in her bathrobe like a newborn in a blanket, passes me. A giant whiff of cigarettes makes me sneeze. She refills her mug of coffee and when she passes again, I hold my breath until she slides the door to the deck.

Yoplait!

I freeze like a sprinter ready for a race and listen for confirmation that Yoplait's taken off outside.

"Yoplait," Mom says, with zero urgency.

Unbelievable! I dart toward the door, which is only open about five inches.

"Mom, how could you let her get out again?!" I say too short and then add more softly, "I reminded you about this yesterday."

I cross the deck in a few steps, but Yoplait's already on the grass.

The problem with cats who think they're dogs is that they're faster than you'd guess, even the kind with a swinging belly.

"Yoplait, come back!" Sprinting, I chase the furry blur through our backyard, across ginormous empty land and right onto the neighbor's property.

"Stop that cat!" I shout, though there's no one around. "C'mon, Yoplait!" She's after the neighbor's dog. Again. "Leave that dog alooone!"

Fudgsicles! Yoplait dodges precious late summer blooms and tears up the moss. Great. This is Street O' Old People and old people get funny about kids running through their yards.

Dirt squishes between my toes. I hop in a crazy obstacle course. Careful. Left. Right. Left. Left. Right.

The Chihuahua slips through a hole no bigger than Yoplait's head and into the safety of her fenced yard.

"Yap! Yap! Yap!" she shrieks and her mini body inches backward.

Yoplait's flat-ish face is pressed against the wire fence. "Grrrrr," she bellows. Her puffed up peachy body, with a tail double the dog's size, is clearly in attack-mode. She's not a good digger because she's clawless, but she tries anyway.

"Yoooooplait!" I'm louder this time. I stuff my frizzy hair behind my ears and clap my hands. "Come!"

She throws back a surprised look, as if suddenly realizing I am there. Trotting to me, her tail deflates and wags.

"Yap! Yap! Yap! Yap!"

Easy on the drama, Chihuahua.

It's our cue to head home.

"Mom just has got to remember to watch for you when she goes out on the deck."

Yoplait's front paws rest on my shoulder, and from the yapping still going on behind us, I'm pretty sure she's still making growling faces. "She knows you can't resist an outside adventure."

I wrap my arms tighter around Yoplait and walk on the grass because bare feet on a dirt road is a bad idea. She purrs like when she hears someone, even two rooms away, peel back the lid on a Yoplait yogurt cup. She's probably the only cat on the face of the planet who'd choose a strawberry banana yogurt cup over fish or chicken.

"Listen, you're an indoors kind of pet." I haven't the heart to tell her she's not a dog. "And I'm going to be real busy this year. So stay inside when Mom goes out on the deck. Okay? I can't be worrying about you."

Her head bobs and I swear it's not a coincidence.

A couple of birds swoop by and Yoplait lets out a meow-growl, which is as close to catlike as she gets.

"Mmmrrrr." More birds. I move Yoplait to rest on my other shoulder, but we're home anyway. I hold her with both arms.

"So, just be good, okay? No more running off. You might get lost. It's nice inside our house, it really is. Dad just has to work a lot. And Mom, she—"

Ouch. Pebbles and bare feet. Bad combo. I kick them from the driveway into the street. When I was little, Mom and I used to collect pebbles and rocks and paint pretty things on them. That was a long time ago.

Amigo raises his head for a second but falls right back to sleep on the lawn. Chasing Chihuahuas isn't something old-man dogs do.

Close to the deck, I think to reprimand Mom again. But she's so tiny on that white lounger, always with a cigarette and glass of wine or bottle of beer, just staring at fireflies and listening to bugs, birds and nothingness. What the heck is she thinking about out here? What is making her feel crummy?

Like closing my eyes on a rollercoaster, I don't

know what's coming next.

"Flipping noodles!" I bend carefully to avoid dropping Yoplait and swat a mosquito who's eating my leg for lunch.

It's always mosquito-y on account of our yard bumping up to woods.

I skip talking to Mom and step across the front porch. Creak creak creak. I've always liked it because it's L-shaped, even though it's noisy. Come to think about it, we haven't sat out here since Dad got the promotion to Executive Director of Production and Quality Control at Maggie Mae Cake Mix Company earlier this year. When you have all those workers to keep in order, you're busy all of the time. He's always at the plant.

Maggie Mae's been around since the beginning of time, so the quality must be perfect or people will get mad and start buying the mix from other companies. Plus, Dad says he needs to work hard to pay off the mortgage on the house. It's big for just Dad, Mom, Yoplait, Amigo, Cindy (my goldfish) and me. It's a solid old farmhouse, despite creaky floors, at least that's what Dad says.

The first thing you'd notice about my room is that the walls are blah-blah beige. Mom says painting them is too big of a project, even though I've offered to do every bit of it myself (except climb a ladder...it just seems that my chicken legs and a gallon of paint and a ladder wouldn't mix well).

On the left are my two tall bookcases that we put together (with no tools!) on a day that Mom was feeling happy. They pretty much cover an entire wall to hold all of my books, snowglobes (from Grandma Dottie) and random things I love like a heart-shaped rock and cheesy predictions about my future on tiny pieces of paper from Chinese fortune cookies.

Against the next wall is my white dresser and on top is Cindy's bowl. Next is my bed, which is smack against the wall on the right, but it's short so it doesn't block my skinny window. My comforter is lilac with sparkles that magically never fall off, even though it's been washed hundreds of times. It's from Grandma Dottie so I'll love it forever. Plus, Yoplait knows the extra cushiony parts that make a good pillow for her head.

Jelly smudges are sticky on my shirt, so I decide to change into around-the-house clothes—stuff from my older cousins with blueberry popsicle-drip stains and stuff like that on them. I slide out of my pants and shirt and stare in the mirror attached to my closet door. It's common knowledge that summer is when everyone grows and comes back looking older. Swollen mosquito bites for boobs are fine for sixth grade. But seventh grade? Man! I pull a white training bra over my head and drop my arms to my sides. And my arms are as twiggy as my legs!

With my nose a few inches from the mirror, I study

my noticeably round, cantaloupe-shaped head. My ears stick out more than they should on a girl. Seriously. It's a problem. And I used to be able to count the freckles on my cheeks and nose, but they've multiplied over the last few summers. It looks like sand fell from the sky and tattooed my face. And for sure my nose is still way too big for my face. Maybe this year, I'll grow into my nose and ears. That'd be awesome. Then there are my eyelashes, which are orangier than my strawberry blond hair and really stand out against my super pale skin and green eyes. When I was little, Mom told me that people spend a lot of time gluing on fake lashes that aren't even as pretty, long and curled as mine. Well, they look like centipede legs to me.

In sweatpants two inches too short and a tank top with dancing monkeys printed on it, I rest against my headboard and update Operation Cool. I like writing in a notebook more than typing on a computer because I can keep it close to me.

There were a heck of a lot more highlights than lowlights on the first day, because of Wreni Hammer. At the top of the Status page, I write, "Day One: Kinda Okay" and report every single thing that happened.

When I finish, I put the notebook away inside my nightstand drawer beside stacks of my photos. I printed like a hundred of my favorite ones from this summer. I spent almost every day taking photographs of everything from close-ups on flowers to the lake to

Main Street (Dad came with me that time, of course). I got pretty good at adjusting the camera's settings based on the sunlight and how I wanted the photo to feel. These photos would never interest anyone else in the world, but I love them. Grandma Dottie bought me a camera after school got out last year because I was always commenting about cool photography in magazines and on TV. Photos show something that happens in a flicker of a second that I probably would never have noticed if the camera hadn't captured it forever. I like the shots taken when people aren't expecting it. That makes it more real and honest—right when you're thinking there's nothing special about the moment, the photo can make something entirely ordinary, extraordinary. In these images, you can see a glimmer of unhappiness in someone's fake smile or total joy in someone's very serious face.

After I spend a few hours taking silly photos of Amigo and Yoplait, I go down and start dinner. Macaroni and cheese, salad and Shake 'N Bake chicken. I've gotten pretty good at making dinner; it's easy if you follow the package directions.

Like I do every night, I find Mom's almost-empty bottle of wine and hold it upside down over the sink. I watch the trickling drops hit the steel and run the water down the side to wash them away.

In the garage, I wrap the bottle in five grocery store bags and slide it between three garbage bags stacked snugly inside of the can.

When Dad comes home at quarter to eight, I'm setting out the salt-and-pepper shakers.

"Hi, honey, you're sure good at setting the table!" he says.

Since Mom usually only makes simple stuff like Shake 'N Bake anyway, Dad doesn't realize that I'm the one cooking it.

I smile, twist the edge of my shirt and shake away the guilt for not telling the truth.

His grin takes up his whole face, from ear to ear, and wrinkles up the skin around his eyes. It's the kind of unique smile that people remember. The ceiling's long fluorescent rectangular light makes the silver at the edges of Dad's blond hair sort of shiny.

"Yep." I nod and place a few napkins in the center of the table.

He smells like sweat and the Maggie Mae plant. It's stinky but it's the smell he's always had when he comes home from work. I've known it forever like the softness of my pillowcase.

"Sue?" Dad calls. He waits a second, and then marches upstairs when there's no response. My heart drops. Come on, Mom. Don't let Dad know you've been drinking.

I listen to his footsteps on the staircase and in the hallway.

"Sue, you're in bed already?"

I tune him out and start spooning mac and cheese onto three plates.

"Mom has a terrible headache?" Dad asks when he returns to the kitchen. He's deep in thought when he stoops and pets Amigo. I don't say anything. "She looks ill."

"You know that flu's going around," I say, real confident. "People at school have it."

He nods without looking at me.

What ifs run through my head, like if he rummaged through the garbage and found Mom's wine bottle. From tonight. And the beer bottles from last night. And the night before. And the night before that night. And last week.

She'll get better soon. Whatever is wrong will just go away; it's got to.

When Dad goes to the bathroom down the hallway, I tiptoe to Mom and Dad's bedroom.

I grip the doorknob and turn softly to open the door wide and take a step forward. Mom's all bundled under their comforter patterned by tiny blue and yellow flowers. When she snores, her hair flutters across her face. Sunset light frames the window, peeking over the edge of the blinds.

"Mom," I whisper. "Please get better soon."

I cover Mom's plate with tinfoil. While I'm setting it on the counter, just in case Mom gets hungry later, Dad returns, sits down and scoots in his chair at the table. At first, you might think he's a real tough guy, since he's tall with wide shoulders and strong arms.

But his round green eyes (the same kind I have) are friendly when you look closely.

Dad half sighs, but it's not loud enough for me to hear. I can only tell because his shoulders go up a little and then down really fast.

"I'm going to be working late at the plant this week," he announces as I sit across from him. "They've doubled the orders." He shakes his head and shovels in his fork carrying a tall mound of mac and cheese.

"Okay." I line up three macaronis side by side and stab them with my fork.

"Mmmm!" He grins like it's the best mac and cheese he's ever had. "Delicious!"

I nod.

"So, tell me all about the first day of seventh grade!"

I can't disappoint him, so tell him all about school, including Wreni and how I don't know what to think about her.

"Sounds like she thought you were great!"

This is annoying to me, though it shouldn't be, and then I feel bad for feeling annoyed.

"Well, maybe, but I don't know what's up with it. Maybe she's a jerk. I dunno yet."

There's no point. He's convinced I've found a friend. Always jumping to conclusions and thinking he's right about everything. And thinking he's listening but he's really not. That's Dad.

I push the chicken around until it's soaked in cheese sauce.

"What was Mom doing when you got home from school?"

"I don't remember." I shrug and clear my throat.

"Easter?" He says slow and paused.

I swallow one too many noodles and cough. Noodle. Stuck. In. Throat. Amigo barks from the living room like, 'Are you okay?'

"Put your arms in the air!" Dad orders, army general style.

I stand and shoot both arms up into the air. My chair tips back. Bam! It hits the sliding glass door just as the noodle in my throat settles and slips down to where it's supposed to be.

When I sip my glass of water, drips roll off the end and land on my t-shirt. I run my hand over it as if that has some kind of drying ability. Dad hands me the towel that was folded over the oven door handle. I nod to say thanks and Dad puts his dish in the dishwasher.

"Chew your food carefully," he says, like I'm four.

Before heading to the basement to "catch up on the exploding inbox," Dad squats so he's eye level with Amigo and gives him four pats on his head. Amigo's tail wags like a wiper across a windshield in a rain shower. He's a very happy animal.

For a second, I wish I were a dog, or a cat who thinks I'm a dog. But then I figure they probably worry, too.

I rinse my dish and rest it beside Dad's in the dishwasher.

I just need to focus on Operation Cool. Day Two. In less than twelve hours.

At two thirty three a.m., my bedroom door creaks and opens halfway, sending a thick band of hallway light into my room.

I'm out of half-sleep land right away; I rub eyes so I can see in the light.

"Mom?" I whisper, even though I already know it's her.

She takes a few steps forward, and from the way she moves—steady and gentle—I know she's not drunk anymore.

Yoplait's snoring stops and beside me, she flops her body over to confirm that it's Mom and not some intruder like Drama Chihuahua or someone else not welcome here.

"Mmm hmm," Mom says. It sounds like her. Nice Mom. The Mom I love.

I move my legs a bit so that there's enough space for her to sit on my bed.

Mom runs her fingers over the spot and sits.

"What's wrong, Mom?"

After about ten seconds, she says, "Nothing, sweetheart." Though she tries to make it convincing, the words feel empty and untrue. "Just making sure you're warm enough. Temps went down tonight."

She pulls my comforter up over my shoulders.

"I'm fine," I say as upbeat as I can. "But I haven't been able to sleep real well lately."

"Sometimes," she says, looking away from me now. "It's difficult to tell your body what to do. Sometimes you lose control."

I have no idea what that means, so I don't say anything.

"I'll sit here until you fall asleep," she says.

It's just like when I was little.

So I turn on my side and face Yoplait, who's already back to sleep. I can tell because her tail is wagging—just a little. That means she's dreaming of yogurt cups and running Chihuahuas out of town.

Mom leans forward and draws on my back, just like she always did.

Hearts. Trees. Butterflies. Flowers. Ice cream. Everything happy drawn gently on my t-shirt.

And I sleep.

• • • THREE

Lemony cleaning solution smells punch me in the nose as I squat at my locker to organize my folders beside the textbooks.

I'm deep in thought about tomorrow. I'll wake up extra early and make breakfast for Mom so that she'll get up before I leave for school.

"Achoooo!" My sneeze comes long, loud and without warning, so I barely have my mouth covered in time to catch the mess. It could've landed on the shoe of the kid next to me!

Don't goof up Day Two.

"Excuse me," I mumble, with one hand covering my mouth until I can fish out a travel tissue from inside my old blue-and-green plaid backpack.

With a tissue folded over my nose, I lean in as close to my locker as I can get without actually stepping inside of it. I'm blowing it and wiping super polite because that is what ladies do.

A loud "hey!" comes from my right and I nearly fall over. Wreni's bending to see what the heck I'm doing down here.

"Ha!" I say aloud, as if that makes sense.

"What's up?" Wreni asks, straightening her striped ribbon headband.

"Oh, nothing," I nod and stuff my tissue into my pants pocket as fast as I can. "Just sneezed this crazy sneeze." Why would she care about that? Yeesh.

Wreni waits for me to grab my book and stand.

As we move into the crowd, Horse Girl steps in front of me. "Wreni!"

I want to roll my eyes, but I never actually would.

"Hey." Wreni nods.

"So whatdya think so far?" Horse Girl smirks and rolls her eyes, like 'We're better than everyone here.' "This place blows, right?"

Wreni shakes her head like 'no.' "Gotta keep your mind open. I'd be pretty stupid to judge this place after one day."

Horse Girl's jaw tightens and she nods. The air feels super uncomfortable, so I step around Wreni. But she steps forward at the same time and we bump each other's arms.

"Oh, sorry!" I say, at the exact same time she does!

Pretty much every head in the classroom turns

toward Wreni when she enters.

It's not that she looks that much older than us; it's the way she walks like she's seen more exciting things, only not in a really stuck up way or anything.

We haven't had a new kid for a while, but I don't remember anyone who wasn't already figured out by Day Two. I mean their coolness level and stuff.

I get the feeling everyone's like, 'What's up with Wreni Hammer?'

"Goood morning!" Mrs. Martin says at her podium in the corner of the classroom. The way she says 'good' is so extra deep and loud, I wonder that if you only heard her voice, you might think she's a man.

Someone mumbles, "Morning" and two people sigh.

"Most teachers like to skip over a day like today, but I guess I'm cooler than that."

Blank stares. Mrs. Martin chuckles.

"Today is my birthday!" She points to red and white roses in a tall vase on the left corner of her paper-stacked desk, as if the flowers are proof that she's not making it up.

"How old are you?" Tommy Hansen asks.

Mrs. Martin shoots him a total 'were-you-raised-in-a-barn' look. "Never ask a lady her age, Thomas." She holds the look for a second so he knows not to make that mistake again. "So, anyway, I brought cupcakes!" She claps her hands like she's just made our day.

"And…" Wait for it. We all know this will mean she's cooked up some sort of assignment that makes her happy and us miserable. "I've decided that since it's so sunny and warm, we can go outside to journal today!" Then Mrs. Martin changes her voice to sound all kid like and shouts, "This class is a piece of cupcake today, right?!" Her quiet giggle explodes into a deep chuckle.

Oh, Mrs. Martin.

I smile at her because it's nice that she made the cupcakes to share with us. Maybe she didn't have anyone to make cupcakes for her.

And they are pretty amazing-looking cupcakes.

They're frosted in your choice of red, turquoise or yellow—her favorite colors—and each topped with some kind of interesting something-or-other.

In the grassy area outside of the doors, Mrs. Martin places the trays atop the picnic table reserved for "the administrators" and we stand around them.

Tommy Hansen picks a yellow one with a flat baseball on top.

I pick a yellow frosting one, too, but with a turquoise butterfly that has heart-shaped wings decorated with purple polka dots. The details! The butterfly sparkles so much in the sun, I'm sure it's made of solid sugar! Almost too pretty to eat! Most teachers don't like to give kids sugar. Then again, we're sorta not kids anymore, so bravo, Mrs. Martin. You'll get some cool points for this.

Under my favorite tree, a huge Weeping Willow, I kneel and run my hand over the grassy dirt to make sure it's dry and then sit, Indian style, with my cupcake and set my notebook down beside my shoes.

"Can I sit here?" Wreni points to the space between me and the tree trunk.

"Sure!" Seriously? She wants to sit with me?

She smoothes her shorts, sits with her knees bent, and leans against the tree.

I'm searching for something to say when she whispers, "What's up with that Erica Morski girl?" One of her eyebrows like two inches taller than the other.

I freeze. "Ooh," I whisper. "I dunno." What is she getting at?

"Does she say jerky stuff all of the time like she did yesterday?"

I suck in a deep breath. "Yeah, she's sort of like that." I pull my pencil from the spiral part of the notebook. "Mostly to me."

Wreni grits her teeth. "I could tell by her bad aura!"

Then this flies out of my mouth before I can even think:

"It started in the third grade when her best friend Stephanie got sick of her always wanting to do what she wanted to do and bossing everyone around. And Stephanie and I got along real well and then they sort of didn't hang out anymore. I think she was mad about that."

Wreni throws her arm up in the air and her bracelets cling and clang together. "That's not your fault! What a jerko."

Something about the way she says jerko really cracks me up.

"In the fifth grade, out here on the grass, I was walking by Horse Girl and her crew who were making up some kind of dance. I was moving fast to avoid her as much as possible when I tripped. Scratch that. She stuck out her foot so that I would trip. I stumbled into two other girls. This caused one of them to bump Horse Girl, too, and she lost her balance and fell against a bush with pokey things, sending a bee cyclone around all of us." A couple of kids sit a yard away so I lower my voice. "Turns out, Horse Girl's allergic and the sting sent her to the hospital. Her version of the story, of course, is that the domino crash was caused by my clumsiness."

Wreni shakes her head. "Oh, her karma is in trouble!"

"Well, it's not so bad anymore. I mean I just ignore it all."

"Why," she says, rather than asks. "You shouldn't ignore it."

"I mean part of it is my own fault. It's been two whole school years since my one and only best friend Stephanie moved away." Still stings when I think about it. "From third grade until she left at the end of fourth grade, we were sort of in our own world. We really didn't hang out with anyone else. Then when she left, I was sort of by myself, you know. Everyone already had their groups of friends."

Earth to Easter! Hellooo? Just shut up. Seriously. Just stop talking mid sentence. That wouldn't be half as bad as your rambling right now.

Wreni just stares at the dirt.

Great. You said too much!

To shut myself up, I take a giant bite of the cupcake—right into the sugary butterfly. I bite hard but can't break the butterfly, so I do what any flustering seventh-grade nerdo would do. I push the whole butterfly into my mouth. Chomp. Chomp. It echoes deep inside my ears.

"There were people like her back in Chicago," Wreni says, all serious, and puts her cupcake down on the grass to shred blades of grass into a tiny pile.

What's wrong with this butterfly thing?! Why isn't it breaking into a thousand pieces? What kind of candy is this, anyway? Once it's lying flat atop my bottom row of teeth on the right side, I crunch my top row of teeth over it.

Chomp. Nothing. Chomp. Nothing.

"In the fourth grade, I was dealing with some ridiculously jerky wannabe divas," Wreni says. "And once I didn't give dog doo about it, there was no drama and they got bored and stopped talking about me."

"Oh, mmm hmm." I nod. The butterfly's plastic!

Panic! Panic! You idiot! Now she'll think you're the stupidest person ever! If I pull it out of my mouth in a quick motion, there'll be a spit trail a yard long and Wreni will be like, 'EWWW! What are you doing?'

"Uh huh," I say again, nod and shift the butterfly from the right to the left side of my mouth and back.

Wreni pauses. "People are dumb, you know? You have to just be like, 'I don't care' and be cool with yourself."

I nod again. She looks at me for longer this time, takes a bite of her cupcake and pulls the white smiley face from her mouth and sets it on her knee.

She stares at my fat right cheek. "Ha, that's weird. Your butterfly was sugar? Mine's plastic."

I freeze, lower my head and pull it out of my mouth as fast as I can. Spit dripping. There's nothing to say that wouldn't make it worse.

My face burns. My arms lock. "No, it's plastic," I confess.

She giggles, which bursts into laughter, and she leans forward, almost dropping her cupcake.

"Easter! That's hilarious!"

I force a quick laugh, but she can tell I'm embarrassed, which only makes it more embarrassing, because she tries to quiet her laughing by looking away and covering her mouth.

"Ladies?!" Mrs. Martin passes us and motions a cut-it-out with her hand over her neck, and this ends the conversation.

We both open our notebooks and write.

The wet butterfly rests in the dirt…spit glistening in the sunshine. Who ever heard of stinking polka dots on a butterfly anyway?

"The best ice cream flavor is peppermint," I tell Dad on the way to Scoops after school. "It tastes like Christmas and summer mixed together."

Dad had been working at the plant until like eight or so every night so I'm surprised when he picks me up.

"I just thought I've been working so many long hours, maybe I should leave a little early today," he says. "Plus, I was craving ice cream and thought you'd be up for it."

"For sure, Dad!" I give him my biggest smile, but worry blankets me. Jell-O dominoes! What's Mom up to at home? If Dad comes home early, she better be in an okay condition. What about dinner? Crapola.

Scoops is the coolest after-school hangout for Lake of Eileen kids, especially for the seventh and eighth graders. It's between Lake of Eileen Lanes and Barbara's Floral. Kids walk there after school. MINUS their parents. Of course, Dad would never let me go there without a grownup. I know it, even though I haven't ever been invited to go by anyone.

Scoops is unique because it's done up like a 1950s ice cream parlor with hot pink walls, a real working jukebox, spinney stools and vinyl records hanging by fishing wire from the ceiling. Plus, there's a whole rack of candy with the old-fashioned kinds you can't get at the gas station.

For a second, I'm excited to be part of the scene. Then I remember: I'm walking in with my dad. Twenty gazillion times worse, I'm walking in with the guy who's probably their parents' strict boss, since pretty much everyone's parents work at Maggie Mae.

My heart sinks and I think about making up some whopper about having a stomachache suddenly. I decide not to because it might hurt his feelings.

Nothing's worse than bringing a grownup to an after-school hangout. They'll think he's eyeing them for suspicious behavior or memorizing their faces. He has that tough guy look, too, you know, despite the friendly eyes.

Everyone turns when the bells jingle above the entrance. I walk a few feet behind Dad, hoping people might think I'm a girl who just happened to walk in behind Maggie Mae's quality control police. Some stare at us, even though he's not wearing a Maggie Mae jacket or anything. Even if he's not their parents' boss, they probably recognize him from the company picnics and all the hoopla in the township's newspaper when he got the big promotion and the company announced that they'd hire more workers this fall.

"It's Chief Maggie Mae," mumbles Tommy Hansen. There he is, sitting on the windowsill, sun glowing behind him, and totally staring down Dad.

Butterflies do gymnastics inside my belly.

Two tables of kids lower their ice cream cones and their heads move from side to side in sync from Dad to Tommy and back. Sour blueberries! Please keep walking, Dad.

"Mr. Hansen," Dad says and narrows his eyes like he's searching his memory files for dirt on him. "I trust your brother is doing better."

The brother story!

Last summer, there were rumors about Tommy's high schooler brother who was working at Maggie Mae. He got caught doing drugs at lunch, I overheard someone say, and Dad called the police right away and fired him. I don't know if it's true or not, but it's not like I'm going to ever ask Dad about it.

"Yes, sssssir," Tommy says and gives an aye-aye captain salute, and almost in sync, kids at the two tables cover their mouths, but it doesn't drown out their laughter.

I might melt the ice cream. My face burns at a minimum of one million degrees. Please. Please. Please. Dad, don't cause a fuss.

The girl behind the counter asks for my order, so I pretend to study the rows of flavors under the glass counter. Dad joins me and I breathe. We both order peppermint in a cone. He grins after a big lick off the top. It just has that effect on people, even those who are super serious all of the time.

Then good luck makes its first appearance of the

school year: Dad's cell rings so he steps away to take the call next to the far wall.

I take a giant bite out of my double-scooped waffle cone, and—

"Hey, Easter."

I recognize Connor's voice even before I turn around.

"Hey, what are you doing here?" I ask. Dumb questions like this always echo in my mind, but it's just Connor so I don't care. As much.

"Can't get enough of these." He smiles and holds up a package of ultra-sour jawbreakers.

Jingle jingle.

Through the door comes son-of-a-lima-bean Horse Girl with her hyena laugh, like she just heard the funniest joke ever. Only I know it's her idea of a grand entrance so everyone in the whole place will look up at her.

Connor doesn't turn his head. Like I said, I always thought he was pretty cool.

"Ha, I saw that Mrs. Martin gave you a few of them yesterday," I say, ignoring Horse Girl as she approaches me. "You must have asked her if she had a good summer just to get—"

"You're melting, Wicked Witch," Horse Girl says, followed by more hyena-ness.

"What?"

"Youuu arrre mellltttting," she says, like I'm stupid. She points to the floor where a small peppermint ice cream pool has formed. This cues the laughter of other kids in our grade who've been shadowing her since forever.

"Oh, flipping noodles!" I half smile at Connor and play it smooth.

"Pfff, what a lame-o." Horse Girl looks me up and down, rolls her eyes and moves with her crew to the Order Here sign, under which Dad is facing the counter, still on his cell, saying yes every two seconds.

I grab a wad of napkins from the table next to us and squat at the floor, trying to be real lady-like on account of wearing a black cotton skirt that hits at my knees. Only while I'm down there, balancing the cone in my right hand and wiping the floor with the other hand, big drips run down my wrist and land on my skirt. I get panicky, lose my balance and land on my butt, flashing my yellow undies and creating a double-scoop mess.

"Oh man." Connor's holding back laughter. He puts out his hand to help me up.

Dad slams his cell shut. He scans the room and misses me behind the table. "Easter? Easter honey?!" He hollers before giving me a chance to respond.

"Right here," I say in a normal, inside voice. I take Connor's hand and stand up, empty cone high in the air.

Horse Girl loves it. She whispers and laughs. Then whispers and laughs some more.

A jingle jingle reminds me of the exit.

Gotta get out.

Connor and Dad stoop down to clean up the mess, and I mumble thanks and head toward the door without even helping.

Closing the door, I take a deep breath and blink in the bright sunlight.

"Oh!" I jump.

Tommy Hansen stands near Dad's truck, beside the picnic tables, throwing his cell phone up in the air fifty feet then catching it like no big deal.

"Hey, Easter."

Speech is impossible. Brain can only process this: Gosh, he is so like James Dean from those old-time movies that I watched with Grandma Dottie.

"Listen, don't worry about that ice cream thing." He nods toward Scoops and shows off his perfect teeth. "It was cute, actually."

"Ha." It's the only thing I can think to say. My heart pounds so loudly, I'm glad my legs are solid stiff and I can't move closer.

"Really." He adjusts his baseball cap so there's no shadow over his eyes. He squints in the sun and then he says, all soft, "Uh, and don't let Erica get to you. She's got a weird sense of humor, you know?"

There's no telling if my ability to speak has returned because the jingle jingle interrupts and Dad steps into the picture.

"C'mon, Easter Ann." Dad puts his hand behind my back and nudges me toward the truck.

"See ya." Tommy passes Dad in three strides without making eye contact. That's probably a good thing, because if Dad's super power were glares, Tommy would be on the pavement.

I am real quiet on the way home, for obvious reasons. I'm glad he missed Horse Girl's nastiness, because he might've tried to lecture her in front of everyone, asked me a gazillion questions and gotten the school involved.

Besides, he'll have enough to get mad about if Mom's in bad shape at home.

• • • FOUR

Dad doesn't speak while he scans the living room and kitchen before marching right up to the sliding glass door.

Mom's not out there.

Come on, Mom. Please don't mess things up.

My heart drops when the stairs creak and Dad calls, "Sue! Hello? We're home."

I sit on the kitchen floor and rest against a cabinet. I don't know why. Yoplait steps onto my thigh and I whisper, "Hey there." She flops her body over my legs, and with her front paws resting on the side of my leg, she waits for me to stroke her head. When I scratch under chin, she closes her eyes tight and stretches her neck as high as it will go. Her tail sweeps across the floor and pushes a Cheerio back and forth before Amigo sees it and gobbles it.

"It seems like she's been sleeping all day," Dad says when he returns to the kitchen. He's deep in thought when he stoops and pets Amigo.

"Remember, I told you that the flu's going around," I say real confident. "A ton of people at school have it."

Without looking at me, he says, "Seems like this has happened a lot recently."

She'll get back to normal. She just needs something to take up her time. She'll feel a lot better soon.

After Dad goes to change the oil in his truck, I tiptoe to Mom and Dad's bedroom.

I grip the doorknob and turn softly to open the door wide. I take a step forward, my hand still holding the doorknob. Mom's all bundled under her comforter again.

"Mom," I whisper. "Please feel better soon." I say fifty prayers right there in the hallway.

"I miss…" I whisper, and then a little louder, "you." Yoplait peeks in and I nudge her back into the hallway with my foot.

I wake to yelling long before my alarm clock's set to go off.

Yoplait, curled up near me in my bed, doesn't raise her head, but her tail wags to let me know that she knows I'm awake. She's too sleepy to get up.

I pull the covers over my head for a really long time. Wouldn't it be genius to invent a new kind of air freshener spray that neutralizes bad smells AND bad noise? It wouldn't just cover it up. In a magical poof, it would turn noise into much happier sounds, for good. Turn the shouting into laughing in one little spray! I'd like that very much.

Between muffled cursing from Mom, I hear Dad—clear and stern—say the worst word in history, ever: Divorce.

I wrap my arms around Yoplait and pull her close. My heart hurts like when Horse Girl teases, only a hundred gazillion times worse.

Dad's work shoes are loud against the kitchen tile. He's leaving extra early.

His job at Maggie Mae is a majorly big deal. Dad has to inspect finished product, ingredients, and materials at all stages of the mix making. One time, he went to some food conference for a week, and I guess some of the workers weren't paying attention, because a while later, some lady found pieces of plastic inside of her cake mix box! Seriously! Can you imagine that? No second chances for sloppy workers, Dad told me, so he tracked down who was responsible for that batch and they got fired! That was even before Dad got the fancy title.

That's why I don't say anything to him about Mom and her, well, troubles. He'd just flip out and if Mom couldn't quickly shape up, maybe he'd say it's hopeless and divorce her. Just like that.

I don't fall back to sleep but wait for the beeping.

I hit the faded off button on my thunderous alarm clock.

Day Three.

Extra alert in an instant, I sit up and fling my covers aside. Amigo, sprawled across my hot pink rug, is on all fours quickly too. He puts his front paws on the bed and kisses my arm in one giant, slobbery lick from my wrist to my elbow.

"Whoa, got some major doggy breath going on today, Amigo." I wrap my arm loosely around his head and give a noogie. "Love ya anyway."

Yoplait yawns a hello and I scratch under her chin.

My door's open just enough for Amigo's nose, which sends it flying with a bump against the wall.

Breakfast is the only time you see him running. I follow him down the hall and stairs, hitting every single creaky part.

When we reach the kitchen, Mom is pouring water into the coffeemaker. She looks at me and fumbles with her favorite kitchen appliance.

"Hi, Mom!" I say, upbeat.

She mumbles "morning" before she shuts the swinging coffee holder, puts the pot under it and presses the button that glows.

"Third day of seventh grade," I say and take a deep breath. "Summer flew by, didn't it?" I pause until she unglues her eyes from the coffeemaker. Should I ask her to straighten my hair? No lion's mane today would be nice. She always liked to help me fix it. Before all of this stuff. Not listening. "Mom?"

Leaning over the kitchen sink, she looks down like she's lost something in the drain. A window-shaped beam of sunshine hits her face like a spotlight. Her eyes are really puffy.

"Yes, Easter," she says slowly and kind of out of breath, like talking to me is the last thing in the world she wants to do.

I'm not sure what I expect her to say. But that definitely isn't it.

Amigo stares at his empty bowl and barks a reminder to Mom but she ignores him. As I pass to the pantry to get the dog food, she steps closer to the sink so we don't bump.

I pour a big heap into his bowl and Amigo gobbles it up.

Mom walks away without a word.

I toast a bagel just right, but I'm hardly hungry, so I take a few bites and wrap the rest.

Upstairs in my room, I lean on my dresser and stoop in close to Cindy's bowl to sprinkle flakes. She swallows them whole, swims up to the glass with bubbles trailing and looks right into my eyes. That's how she says thank you for taking care of me; it's the only way a goldfish knows how to show it.

I spin to stare inside my closet.

Grandma Dottie told me that in New York, Los Angeles and big, fashionable cities like that, people pair vintage pants from a thrift shop with a fancy-schmancy designer shirt with old bead necklaces. Personalities shine! She always says, "You should have seen how glamorous your mama looked in some of the stuff she found buried in my closet!"

I've heard the stories a gazillion times, but I ask Grandma to tell me them again and again. When she was a kid, Grandma tells me, Mom swayed and twirled to rock and roll while singing with a hairbrush microphone in her bedroom. In high school, she worked every day after school at a shoe store in order to pay for guitar and voice lessons. She got so good, that after high school, she landed a role as the lead singer in a band and they were kinda, sorta famous. The band toured all over Detroit, Chicago and other music-loving cities. I've seen the photos of Mom on stage with her hair long and sleek, bright pink lipstick, gobs of mascara, a neon green dress, jean jacket, dangling hoop earrings and about a dozen bracelets on each wrist. She was glamorous, well as glamorous as you could be with the crazy fashion of that decade.

Actually, it's really not hard to imagine Mom rocking out; she still has that superstar prettiness and I've seen how happy she can be. But she hasn't played the guitar, danced or sung a song since I was little.

Briiing.

I'm about to go to check the caller ID when Mom shouts up the stairs, "Do not answer it!"

"Okay," I say only to myself.

That means it's Grandma Dottie again. I can't answer her calls when Mom's around.

Last spring, they got into a big argument when Grandma Dottie came for a surprise visit. I was at school so I'm not sure exactly what happened, but it was bad.

Grandma Dottie didn't even come inside the house last time she visited because she thought Mom would get upset. We went shopping at the thrift shop in July and we put together this one awesome outfit: A sleeveless creamy top that she called a blouse with lacy ruffles at the neck that flow down the middle next to pearl buttons. So sophisticated! I could add a broach from Grandma Dottie that she bought back in "who knows what year" before she got married. I like it because it has two rhinestone flowers. It's so classic and elegant with my ruffle-y skirt. I love vintage clothes but they're waaay too different for Lake of Eileen.

Lake of Eileen people shop at the same stores in the same three little cities that surround the town. I'm pretty sure that they just buy whatever's put together for the mannequins. So if you wear unique stuff, you stand out, but not in a good way.

Horse Girl and her killer sense of humor. Gag. Trust me, I know. Best to play it safe around here.

It's a shame, Grandma Dottie would say.

Inside my closet, a pale pink t-shirt hangs beside folded plain jeans that flare a bit at my knees.

Downside: It's not special. Upside: It's safe from snarky Horse Girl comments.

I slide on the boring outfit and spin around on my heels.

"Whaddya think, Yoplait?"

Resting on folded-in paws, she looks like a loaf of peach-flavored bread on the edge of the bed.

She blinks.

"I know," I whisper. "Boring."

I slide on a pair of plain brown sandals and do an Irish jig/tap dance and take a spin near the mirror.

"Maaan. This hair!" I decide not to ask Mom about fixing it. I brush it a few times and make a halo over it with anti-frizz hairspray. I pull it back with a skinny headband and pretend I don't notice that this makes it taller.

Can't be late, anyway.

I put my fancy camera into its soft grey pouch and pack it snugly into the side pocket of my backpack. I might be able to get some nice shots of town on the bus ride. I've always sat by myself on the bus, anyway, so I won't be bugging anyone.

When I close my desk drawer, Operation Cool catches my eye.

"It's totally guaranteed to work," I say, Home-Shopping-Network lady style. My finger accidentally smashes in the drawer as I slide it closed.

"Yow!"

Yoplait jumps to her feet.

"Gotta work on my clumsiness, too."

Downstairs, Mom's curled up on the couch, watching the news on TV.

"Bye, Mom," I say on my way to the kitchen to grab my lunch.

"Bye," she grumbles in the world's groggiest voice.

"Mom, are you sick or something? Got a cold?" I twirl my lunch bag in one hand.

"Nooope," she says all slow.

She rubs her face against the couch pillow and pulls a flowery blanket over her shoulders.

"Oh, okay. Well, I hope you feel…great today."

"Thanks."

I look at her for a few seconds longer. Her eyes are dull. They're the same color brown but somehow different. Like, when you lose hope and happiness in your heart and mind, it has a de-sparkle effect.

Downstairs, my backpack's loaded up with two binders, six notebooks, ten folders decorated with fuzzy kittens and smiley puppies, and a plastic box full of pens, pencils and markers. My legs burn when I squat to pet Amigo and Yoplait.

"Bye, Mom!" I shout with one foot out the door. "Mom, bye!" I call again, after she doesn't respond.

"Bye, Easter," Mom finally says.

"Maybe go and get a coffee in town!" I don't wait for her response. I lock the door behind me and walk to the bus stop at the end of our street.

Come on, Day Three. Don't let me down.

• • • FIVE

Homework that doesn't feel like homework. That's why I love Language Arts class.

Our last assignment was to write about the greatest gift, fancy schmancy or simple, that we ever received and why it was so special.

Naturally, Yoplait popped into my head.

I wasn't expecting a kitten for my sixth birthday, but Grandma Dottie decided that every little girl should have a cat.

"Taking care of it will build character," she said with confidence to Mom, who was as surprised as me but not thrilled at first. But once Mom saw how happy my new friend made me, she let it be. One day she even said, "Love is the hardest emotion to describe but when you love, you just do and you know it. That cat can't understand your words but she knows your heart well." I'll always remember that.

In my essay, I wrote about how Yoplait is the greatest gift I've ever received because it's not often you get a best friend for a birthday present. I also wrote about how she's not a dog but I don't have the heart to tell her otherwise, that she knows more tricks than Amigo, how she always listens to my stories and how Drama Chihuahua is on her watch list.

It really wasn't all that interesting, but I guess I strung the sentences together okay, because the teacher says it was one of the best. In front of the whole class, of course! And before I can react, she puts the paper back into my hands and asks me to read it aloud.

"Listen to the great details Easter included, class," she instructs.

I let gravity slink me lower in my chair. If she weren't a newer teacher—much younger and perkier than Mrs. Martin—I would say I'd rather not, but I don't want to hurt her feelings.

Crrrrhhh. My stupid, weird, throat-clearing sound echoes in the room.

I'm only a paragraph in when I hear snickering in the back of the classroom. Please let it be that someone farted or something. But they keep it up until the teacher does a cut-it-out signal, but that only quiets them a tad. Horse Girl's muffled hyena-ness stabs inside my ears.

After class, Wreni beats me to door and whispers,

"Good job!"

I half smile.

On the way to my locker at the end of the day, TOMMY HANSEN TAPS ME ON MY SHOULDER.

"I like my cat a lot, too," he says totally randomly. "So I liked your essay." He nods back toward the classroom.

"Oh, ha, that's great. Good. Thank you. That's nice. Thanks a lot." Shut up now.

He stares, smiles a little, then a lot and walks away before more words with the same meaning tumble from my mouth again.

I smack my forehead with full force, which makes a noise that causes the kid next to me to look at me like I'm nutso, so I spin around and walk as fast as I can without running.

At dismissal, I stick some of the photos I took of Lake of Eileen in the very back of my locker. As I make little tape rings and press them to the back of the photos, I feel someone standing close, so I step back an inch or two.

Connor tips his head to the side and peeks into my locker.

"Hey, sweet photos." He leans in and squints into the darkness. "Is that...Lake of Eileen?"

"Uh, yeah, sunset one night over the summer."

"Whoa. If I didn't know Lake of Eileen, I'd think it

was paradise. Like from a travel website or something. Where'd you get those?"

"Oh, I took them," I say casually as my face gets hot.

"Get out."

"Yeah, I did." I nod, reach in and press the last photo against it and smooth it out with the palm of my hand.

"Easter, they're awesome." He gets closer, so I step aside and his smile widens and dimples appear. "Seriously, they're magazine quality."

"Nah." I shake my head. "I have a decent camera and the lighting was good."

"Take a compliment, Easter Peters." He punches my shoulder in slow motion.

"Yes, okay, they're total masterpieces." I roll my eyes. Taking photographs won't make you cool. "It's not a thing." I swing my backpack onto one shoulder. "Just a hobby, I guess."

"Photography's cool," he says. "Kind of freezes time. Like Ferris Bueller said, 'Life moves pretty fast. If you don't stop and look around once in a while, you could miss it.'"

"Who's Terris Mueller?"

"Seriously?" His eyes bug out. "80s movie?"

I must have a blank look on my face, because he says, "It's classic! You have to see it."

"Okay," I say as he half waves and walks backward, right into the path of Mrs. Martin, who gives him a watch-where-you're-walking glare.

Then I remember his locker is in the other hallway, closest to the exit, and wonder why he even came back this way at all.

• • • SIX

When I get home, Mom's napping.

I decide to ride my bike down to the lake and feed the sunfish. I put two slices of bread in a sandwich bag and stuff it in my jeans pocket. Then I buckle my helmet, of course. The last thing I need is for Dad to come home early (to check on Mom), catch me helmet-less and launch into another lecture about the importance of wearing one.

The lake sparkles, it really does. There are thousands of baby waves that go in different directions and each one catches the sun and shines.

"It's like one ginormous blue diamond," I told Mom a few weeks ago. But she doesn't think much of it. She says the lake is nothing more than fish poo and weeds that tangle in your legs. I wish she'd see the good in stuff a little more clearly.

Sometimes she does. While fixing my hair for Picture Day in the first grade, Mom said, "You are a gift to the world because you're beautiful on the inside and on the outside. But the inside is most important."

At that very moment, she put a purple barrette at the side of my head. I didn't like it one bit so I stomped my foot down and shouted, "It makes me look like a baby!" Her feelings looked hurt because maybe she was trying to have a nice talk with me and I went and ruined it.

Sometimes, I think about that. I should have been nicer.

I pedal down our street toward the road that runs right along the north shore of the lake. I love my spot: a little patch of grass between the road and the lake. The sunfish are a lot like Cindy, only bigger and not as pretty, on account of their grayness. I have a routine: I lay my bike down on its side as far from the road as possible, kneel down and pull out the bread. Fish can't smile, but they let you know they're happy to see you when they make eye contact and swarm together. Big and little, they fight for the best spot by bumping into each other.

I usually break off a dime-sized piece of bread and toss it into the water. After an ultra-fast scrambled fight, it'll all be gone. The fastest always wins. After a few throws, I usually notice which little guys didn't get any. I'll distract the fast ones with two pieces in opposite directions and then feed the ones that didn't get any.

When all of the bread is gone, I will say goodbye and head back home, feeling kind of sad that I can't take them out of the smelly water and give them a giant bowl like Cindy's with colorful pebbles and a castle to swim in.

As I near the lake, I notice that it's extra sparkly and there are a few water skiers out. How amazing it'd be to try that sometime, even though Dad says it's far too dangerous. There are also a few pontoon boats out there, which are basically floating living rooms full of people having fun.

What's way more noticeable is Horse Girl standing there in MY SPOT with two girls named Rachel and Megan. They're not related but they're pretty much the same person, except Megan always seemed like she'd be alright if she wasn't always Horse Girl's shadow.

Horse Girl feeds the fish, too? I think about going home, but I can't shake the nagging worry/curiosity inside of me. Once I reach the road—squeak! I guess I hit the brakes too hard. The girls spin around.

Talk!

"Hey!" I shout as friendly as possible.

They turn together.

"Hi," they all mumble at the same time and face the water again.

"Oh my God, they're sooo stupid," Rachel says as she stoops to pick up stones.

Horse Girl tosses them in gently. Glunk. Glunk.

Then they point at the water and laugh!

I get off my bike, put my hands on the bars, check for traffic in both directions and cross. This is important to do because every now and then someone on a motorcycle cruises by at a crazy fast rate.

"Hey, what are you guys doing?" Stay cool.

Silence.

When I reach the spot, I drop my bike and a little bit of dirt kicks up and sprinkles across Rachel's sandal. She looks down and then up at me.

"Whoa," she says with a sour face.

Horse Girl copies. Then rolls her eyes and flicks her hair behind her shoulders.

"Sorry," I say as Rachel picks up stones from the strip between the grass and the road. Dirt settles between my toes when I shuffle one flip-flop back and forth.

The fish still gather. They probably think, "Four Easters with bread? It's our lucky day!" This picture in my head officially ticks me off.

Horse Girl throws more stones in, not gently but like torpedoes that scatter the fish in a million directions. Then the fish form a wide circle. They're too confused and scared to cluster together again.

"Stop!" I shout. "That's so mean!"

The girls look at each other and burst into hysterics.

"For real," I say in a softer voice. "That's not cool."

"Theyyy aarrrre FEEEESSSSH!" Horse Girl says, like I'm dumber by the second.

"Yeah, I know, but they're expecting bread." I wave the bag of bread high in the air. "I feed them."

"C'mon, seriously?" Rachel asks.

Horse Girl shakes her head with a Grinchy smirk.

"Yeah, it's kinda fun." I use my best sweetheart voice. "So just don't do that, k?"

"Oh, yes, Miss Peters, we completely forgot that you own this body of water," Horse Girl says, emphasizing a "t" sound whenever possible in the worst fake British accent I've ever heard. Rachel and Megan hold back a major crack up on account of my face growing red and mad and nervous.

"I'm just saying." Be brave. I swallow and it's loud. "You probably wouldn't want anyone to throw rocks at your horses so it should be the same thing, you know?"

"You're a total freak, Easter Ann Peters." Horse Girl makes a crazy person circle motion near her head with her finger. "They are stupid little fish with teeny brains. Guess you've got a lot in common." Then she turns to the other girls to make sure they are finding it hilarious, too, but their faces aren't smiley anymore.

A car zooms by and we bunch closer to the water.

"Come on," Megan says, while stepping close to the road. "Let's just go back to your house, Erica."

The two cross the street without checking traffic, leaving Horse Girl standing there with a permanent pfff look on her face.

I kneel down, pull bread from the bag and pray

Horse Girl will leave. And she does.

"Later, Lame-o." She runs to catch up with the girls.

At first, the fish are really skittish. Can't blame them. When you lose trust in someone, you really don't feel quite right for a while. Fortunately, the big guys are happy to be testers and they gobble up the first helpings. "Guinea pigs!" I whisper. Once all of the fish are convinced it is in fact soft gooey bread, things go back to normal. I break the slices into really tiny pieces so that more can go around.

I head home, proud of myself for defending the fish.

The feeling fades once I find Mom still napping. She's curled up on the bed in a ball and there's a half full glass of red wine on the nightstand and a couple of beer bottles on the floor. They are empty, I know, because they are on their sides, not very neatly.

I wrap them in Lake of Eileen Market bags. This time, though, I lift and pull out three stinky garbage bags by tight red strings, place the bottle bags at the bottom and bury them with the stinky bags.

Grownups are always talking about kids going through "phases." When a kid is getting in trouble a lot at school, his mom will tell the teacher that the kid's just going through a "phase." I guess it's a short little bit of time in which a person acts completely different, shocking everyone around them.

So is this just a phase for Mom? How long do grownup phases last?

• • • SEVEN

"What are you doing for Halloween next week?" Wreni leans against my neighbor's locker.

I don't respond right away because I'm trying not to look overly excited.

"My parents decided that they'll take my brother and me to the Halloween celebration on Main Street," she says. "As a family." She rolls her eyes. "Which means we'll probably be yawning two minutes into it, but if you don't already have plans, it'd be awesome if you could come with."

"Sure!"

"Okay, cool!" She hands me a sandwich bag that holds a sugar cookie with tiny orange bats sprinkled over a perfectly smooth layer of black frosting. "If you had said no, I would have been majorly bummed."

"Yeah! Sure! That sounds great." I hold the bag

close. She brought me a cookie?! "Thanks!"

Operation Cool, whadya think of that? Hey hey hey!

I'm so excited I jump up the bus steps.

"Well, you're peppy today!" the driver says.

Then I come home to no one.

I discover that the front door's locked after I get off the bus and really have to dig to find the key in one of those hidden inside pockets of my backpack.

"Mom?" It feels strange to be in the house alone, even though I'd been home alone other times. This time is different because I didn't expect it; Mom is always home.

Amigo meets me in the kitchen, jumps up, wags his tail and then sits and stares at me like he's been worried, too. Yoplait meows hello from the top of the staircase, stretches her front legs and meets me at the bottom.

This cues the little girl inside of me.

No note. I check every room and the garage in the back. I am having a silent panic attack when I hear Mom's car in the driveway.

When I meet her in the garage, before I can even ask, Mom says ultra fast, like a kid who gets caught drawing with markers on the hallway wall, "I had to just run to the store, Easter. Thought I'd beat you home."

"No big deal," I say grownup-ish, though I really

want to ask what kind of store it was, since she doesn't have a shopping bag.

I follow Mom into the house with a lousy feeling running through me and decide the only thing to do is try to talk to her. Like just talk to her and put it all out there.

Amigo seems hungry, so I grab the bag of dog food and head to the bowl to fill it. Mom steps out of the way, lights a cigarette and curses at Yoplait while scooting her away from the sliding glass door.

"Yoplait, come." I swoop her up and set her gently on the living room windowsill.

I join Mom on the deck, carefully sliding the door closed behind me. I sit on a white plastic chair and put my feet up on it, wrap my arms around my legs and pull them close. At first, we sit in silence.

"Um, Mom," I say, quietly, hoping she'll look at me. No response. "Mom?" I say, louder.

"What?"

"Why are you so sad and down all of the time?"

"Easter, I'm in no mood for this." She whips her head away and shoos me with her cigarette hand. "C'mon, people aren't rosy all of the time!"

She must feel bad for the way that came out because she looks at me for a few seconds and then says, "It's so hard to explain. You're too young to understand."

"Try me." I smile.

She looks away. "I can't."

I know to leave her alone.

The only thing to do is clean the kitchen real well. I even wipe down the refrigerator shelves.

After I finish my homework, I figure I'll spend what's left of the sunshine taking photos in the backyard.

I play catch with Amigo using his favorite torn-up green ball. He's sprinting around with puppy-like energy because the extra attention's a special treat. I take lots of shots of Amigo smiling his doggy smile as he leaps in the air.

Later, I go down to the basement, connect the camera to Dad's computer and open each photo one by one. I adjust the colors and brightness and crop out extra stuff like the deck so you don't see Mom asleep on the deck and so you can notice everything about Amigo, even his whisker moustache.

I run my finger along a frame outlined by pearls that holds a photo of Mom and Dad on their wedding day. They look so young and happy, but so different from each other. Dad's all stiff like he's hoping the photographer's about done, and Mom's relaxed with a huge smile, the real kind, like someone just told her a joke. Sometimes I wonder how they even got together.

Mom and Dad met at one of the band's performances, just after Dad came back from being stationed overseas with the U.S. Marines. According to my dad, he almost didn't go that night, but his friend was a big fan of the band and talked him into it. Mom was so amazing, he was too nervous to talk to her, but she was always real friendly and I guess they finally got to talking enough for Dad to ask her out. I think probably she thought Dad was a lot sweeter than those rock and rollers who were always around her.

After they got married, Dad got the job at Maggie Mae, but Mom wanted to stay closer to Detroit so she could keep singing in the band. So Dad drove back and forth from the city to Lake of Eileen every day.

I'm not sure if it's the only reason, but just after I was born, Mom and Dad moved to a little house in Lake of Eileen, and Mom's music career ended there.

Mom was happy when I was little; I know she was. Dad was working on the assembly line, and because he was a good worker, they quickly gave him an office and more responsibilities, until one day, he was a big shot there.

Why they didn't have any more kids after me, I don't know and I don't want to think about it. I would have been a good sister. Maybe being parents wasn't so exciting and I wasn't really interesting, so they didn't see the point in having more.

"Mom?" I shout down the hallway, from the top of the staircase and then again at the bottom of the staircase. No response.

I find her still out on the deck, lying on the plastic chaise lounger, which has my favorite beach towel draped over it—the one with a giant sunglasses-wearing cat with spiky wet fur on it. It'll be all smoky even after washing it because that's what smoke does—it seeps in, takes over every fiber and then it's never really as great as it once was.

A few feet from the sliding glass door, I watch Mom. She looks pretty relaxed with her legs crossed and her arms folded over her stomach, but the ashtray beside her is brimming over with cigarette butts and her puffy eyes are squinted and focused on the clouds.

For a minute, I wish I could edit life the way I can do with photos. That way, I could crop out the unhappiness. It's deep, I know, but that's how my brain works these days.

In the hallway bathroom, I lean against the counter, which digs into my belly because bellies on string bean girls aren't so cushiony. I notice that my eyebrows are suddenly unbearably bushy. So I open the cabinet door under the sink and find Mom's tweezers in a plastic box full of beauty supplies. I move the tweezers close to my right eyebrow, squeeze and yank one hair out in a fast motion. Yow!

That's it. Can't do it.

They're only semi-medium-thick eyebrows anyway. Yoplait sticks a paw under the door as a 'Yoo hoo,' so I open it and she trots in, checks that the toilet seat is down and jumps up for a seat.

"Hey, girl." I pet her head and under her chin until she gets distracted by the shower curtain and has to inspect it without delay. And while she's walking on the balance beam bathtub edge between the fabric and the plastic curtains, she spots the half-open cabinet door. She lands back on the rug, pulls on the cabinet door with her paw, and it springs open all the way and nearly smacks her in the face.

"Careful, Yoplait." I squat and that's when I see them: three or four beer bottles way in the back of the cabinet behind spongy hair rollers and stacks of soap bars.

Even Yoplait decides not to explore further and jumps back onto the toilet seat.

"Oh no, Mom," I whisper.

Flipping noodles. It's getting worse! My heart spins like I've never felt before. It's not even my stomach this time; my heart hurts in a real way.

The bottles cling clang as I twist off the tops and pour them down the drain.

I wrap them in a raggedy towel and carry them out to the garbage can in the garage.

After I close the door behind me, I tiptoe into the kitchen, but Mom's standing there, with an eyebrow bent.

"Easter?"

"Yes." I nod.

"What did you just have in your hands?"

I ignore her and walk toward to the stairs.

"I asked you a question," she says, like 'You're so in trouble.'"

I stop at the steps and turn around, though I really

want to just run up the stairs as fast as possible.

"Mom, please, get better." I use my sweetest voice so she knows I'm not trying to scold her. "Please, get better."

"You better not've thrown out something of mine."

Stay cool. Don't cry. I drop my hands to my sides and say as calm and grownup as I can. "Mom, why are you doing this?"

I regret it right away when she throws her hands up and stomps her slippered foot to the ground. "I'm fine."

Be brave.

"Mom, I'm sooo worried about you. Please stop this."

For the first time ever, it feels like someone stole her brain and replaced it with another brain. From someone I don't like.

As Dad warms his dinner in the microwave, I scoot a chair from the kitchen table and sit.

"Hi, Easter," he says with fake upbeatness.

My reply gets drowned out by the microwave's it's-ready beep.

I wait until Dad sits and stirs his spaghetti to announce my news. "Got invited to go with the Hammer family to the Main Street Spooky Celebration on Halloween!" I smile my biggest without trying.

Please, please, please. I cross my fingers and my legs, too, under the table.

"The Hammer family?"

"Yes, Wreni Hammer, you know, the new girl I told you about."

"I don't know that family."

"Well, that's because they're new here. Remember?"

"I don't know, Easter." He shakes his head like he's about to make it a flat-out no.

"Why, Dad? It'll be Wreni, her parents and her little brother."

He's thinking. I can always tell because he stares at the tablecloth.

Please, please.

"Well, we'll have to meet the parents before you leave, but I suppose if it's alright with your mother, it sounds fine."

"Yes!"

"What are you going to dress up as?"

Snickering lobsters! I didn't even think about that!

From the back of my closet, I pull out a costume Aunt Deb gave me that she made for some costume party back in college. You might think dressing like a fish is totally weird, but this actually is pretty awesome. No wonder Aunt Deb won first place in the costume contest! It's a light turquoise shirt, square cut at the neck (so no worries that my bra will show!) with a thin layer of shimmery fabric sewn over the front. There are white straps that fit over my shoulders that connect at the back with a foot-long ridge-y plastic turquoise fin that's tightly tied to it by a thick thread. I pair Aunt Deb's plain black skirt with a matching turquoise ruffle along the bottom edge with black leggings and black ballet flats.

Perfect! It feels good to be dressed in something super unique.

• • • EIGHT

On Halloween, after school, Wreni's mom picks us up because I convinced Dad that it'd all be fine and that he could meet them when he picks me up.

Considering that I haven't been to someone's house in about two years, being with another family feels new and strange.

"Oh, hi-ya, sweet Easter! I'm Mrs. Hammer," Mrs. Hammer says before Wreni even has the minivan door all the way open.

Mrs. Hammer's blond hair is feathered high and the light mustache on her upper lip perfectly matches her dark eyebrows. She is plump and dressed in denim covered with tiny fake diamonds lined up to look like flower petals.

"Hi, nice to meet you!"

"So wonderful that Wreni met a great friend like

you." She smiles at the rearview mirror as I settle in my seat.

"Well, I'm just so glad that she's moved here." Understatement.

The Hammers' house is a wide ranch in Lake of Eileen's newest neighborhood full of kids and zero old people. There are skyscrapers of boxes still in the corner of the living room, and everything else about the house is clean—and normal.

Wreni's room is done up with cool posters of bands she likes and a painting of a rose bush that she made in a special art class back in Chicago.

It's so unique, like her.

Wreni changes out of her sweater and skirt and slides into a black leotard suit with a skirt and a sparkly tail.

I majorly feel like a little kid as I slip out of my sweatshirt and jeans and into my fish costume in just a few quick movements.

"You have perfect skin, you brat! Wish I had it," Wreni says.

"Seriously?"

"Yeah! Like a model!"

Wreni wishes she had something I have?

"A fish model." I spin around and we die laughing. "I'm on the fishwalk." I suck in my cheeks and walk like I'm on a fashion show runway. At her dresser, I turn and pose for invisible paparazzi.

Wreni joins me on the fishwalk.

We nearly pass out because when you hysterically laugh, your insides get all twisted up.

"Home!" Wreni's dad shouts from downstairs.

In the hallway outside of Wreni's door, Dustin, Wreni's brother, responds in an unkidlike deep voice, "Look out, sir, here comes Superman!" He sprints so fast down the hall, the frames on the walls shake. Then I hear, "Why are you home early, Dad?"

"I couldn't miss seeing Superman!"

"Cool! Are you going to take our photogwaff?"

"'Course. Where's your sister?"

"We're getting ready!" Wreni shouts from under her flat iron as she straightens chunks of hair, like it's possible to make it straighter. "Be down in a minute!"

Together, we take a spin in the mirror and link arms.

Mr. Hammer, who's thin, tall and bald, smiles at us when we appear the top of the staircase.

"Look, Superman, there's a cat and a fish!"

After Mr. and Mrs. Hammer take fun photos of us on her lawn next to a golden Maple tree, Dustin taps me on my fin.

"You know, together, you and Wreni make a..." He holds back laughter. "Catfish!" Then he falls to the floor, laughing so hard, he has to hold his side.

"Yep, you're pretty smart for a five year old!"

"No, I'm just pretty smart. Period!" More laughing.

Wreni makes crazy person circles around her head

two feet behind him, and this just about kills me.

There's a group of people who own businesses on Main Street who all get together and make a big stink about Halloween. They all get dressed up, like really dressed up. Last year, I saw a walking banana, chocolate chip cookie and grizzly bear, which made me do a double take more than a few times. It was like, "Ahh, what's that?!"

After we've loaded up our Lake of Eileen Market bags with candy from the flower shop, the fitness center, the coffee and tea shop, the car repair place, and the gift store with candles and old-lady sweaters, Mrs. Hammer says, "Oh look! They have Halloween sandwiches and soup!"

"Sweet!" Dustin runs ahead toward the Lake of Eileen Café.

"What makes sandwiches and soup Halloween-y?" I whisper to Wreni.

"I was just wondering the same thing!"

Mr. Hammer's talking to some of the event organizers, so Mrs. Hammer taps him on the shoulder and whispers, "Honey, we'll meet you inside."

He nods and smiles back at her.

So normal.

There are people at every single table and counter stool, but Wreni spots people leaving a booth in the corner so we speed walk to claim it.

As Wreni and I slide in behind the table, Dustin

says, "Mom, I gotta go to the bat-room!"

"Bat-room? You're Superman, not Batman!" Mrs. Hammer says with a tall smirk.

"Mooom." Dustin rolls his eyes. "Battthhhroom."

"Okay, I'll walk you over there."

So Wreni and I are sitting there when the door opens and in walks TOMMY HANSEN. Right there. With a green monster mask resting atop his head. I look at Wreni, but she's already reading the sticky menu.

"Wreni!" I whisper. "Look!"

"I know," she says without looking up.

Before I reach for the menu and pretend to read it, he's there at our table.

"Hey, ladies."

"Haa heey," tumbles out and I twist two napkins in my lap. For the love of all things cool, relax.

"Hi," Wreni says fast and short.

"Cute costumes," Tommy says, pointing to Wreni's whiskers, drawn on with eyeliner.

"Thanks," we say together.

"How'd you do?" He looks at Wreni and then at me.

What? What does he mean? Do what? I scan my brain. Hurry! No results found.

I start to say, "Huhh?" when Wreni puts down the menu.

"Good," she says. "We got a lot of candy."

I nod.

"Saaweet. Me too." Tommy holds up his pillowcase, but it nearly knocks over our waitress who's not dressed for Halloween except for pumpkin earrings.

"Sorry!" Tommy jumps back a foot or two but she doesn't respond, only steadies the round tray and slides it onto the edge of the table.

She places one glass of water on each placemat.

"Thanks!" I say.

When she turns, Tommy steps forward again. "We're gonna go over to North Main. The marina's giving away full candy bars. But last year, the craziest thing happened over there."

I reach forward, rip the paper from around my straw, drop the straw into my glass and crumple the paper into a little ball and hold it in my lap.

"Jake and I saw this dude dressed like a hobo sitting by the water. We went down there to eat some of our candy, and when Jake said, 'Your costume is awesome,' he started shouting at us!" Tommy throws his candy bag over his shoulder, shakes his head, glances around the room to see if anyone's listening and laughs. "He wasn't makin' any sense. Talking about some guy named Johnson, I think. But the rest of it was all babble stuff we couldn't understand. So Jake and I were just standing there like 'What is goin' on?'"

I slide my glass of water across the placemat, soaking it completely, and not wanting to lift a slippery tall glass with my clumsiness problems, I lean forward without taking my eyes from Tommy. I think that my mouth is over the straw, so I lean in more, but it bumps my nose, so I lean back, look at Tommy, and glance back at the glass.

Where's the straw?

In. My. Nose. Panic stops me from pulling it out for at least half a second. It's in my nose!

When I finally grab it and plop it back into my glass, I do it too fast, so it isn't actually in the water all the way when I let go. The straw jumps back out and settles on the table with three mini puddles of water beside it.

Tommy stops and smirks. I look at Wreni, who shoots me a 'get a-hold-of-yourself' look.

Think of something funny to say! Come on! Something! Think!

"So what happened next?" Wreni says, smiles big and looks up like she's into the story all of a sudden. Good old Wreni.

"The guy just kept rambling, so we walked away." Tommy laughs and nods at three eight-grade girls who wave from stools at the counter. "Obviously he wasn't dressed up for Halloween at all."

"Ha!" It's all I can think to say.

Wreni fake smiles.

"Well, see ya, ladies," he says and heads over to sit with the eighth-grade girls.

Wreni and I watch TV with her parents in the living room for a while before Dad arrives and exchanges so-nice-to-meet-you handshakes with Mr. and Mrs. Hammer.

"Have a good time, Easter?" Dad asks when we pull away in his truck.

"Yep!"

I am about to tell him all about it, when he puts two hands on the steering wheel and leans forward a bit like he's got something big to say. "Seems like Mom slept most of the day every day this week."

I bite my lip and rest my head against the window, even though it's freezing.

The silence is going to make him ask more questions, but I don't want to answer.

"What's Mom doing when you come home from school?"

"Normal stuff," I say and count the trees we pass.

"Easter, I sure hope you'll let me know if there's more going on. Is she drinking during the day?"

I cringe at the thought of lying more, but shake my head no so he'll stop talking about it.

• • • NINE

One thing about seventh grade no one warns you about? People cluster tighter together.

Even in the sixth grade, if you walked by the big field after school or on the weekend, you'd see the same group of kids always playing together. At school, same thing. They were always whole, that group of them, at lunch, at gym, at assemblies. They never divided up in twos or threes unless some group project forced it.

In the seventh grade, all of a sudden, there's no big group. There are two and three-person mini groups, and sometimes these mini groups hang with each other, but usually not.

During Advisory (which is supposed to be a study hall, but mostly everyone just checks their email in the library), my class settles in mini-group clusters at long tables.

Wreni has a different Advisory class, so I'm a one-person group.

Okay, perfect time to be a little social so I have something to report on in Operation Cool.

I find a seat between two mini groups, but no one looks my way. They're busy talking, semi hushed.

The media specialist lady claps twice at the book checkout desk. "As a reminder, there is no talking during Advisory." She pauses and stares us down. "Use your time wisely. This is for homework and studying. Understood?"

After she checks the attendance list, she announces that the computers are now open for fifteen-minute blocks of use. All but two people at my table jump up and speed walk to the computer lab attached to the oval-shaped room.

I open my Science binder to the loose-leaf paper page with last night's homework assignment. A kid named Jimmy swooshes by on his way to the computers. I don't notice the note that he leaves atop my binder until he's already out of sight.

That's right. I got noted. Someone took the time to write and prettify a whole letter to me. There's a big "TO" in red gel pen and a giant "E" all fancy. It's folded into eighths and covered in pink and purple flowers and squiggles.

I stick the note up my sweater sleeve in a rush and wait until the media specialist returns to her post at the checkout desk. I lift my books, hold them close and relocate to a spot in the corner by a dusty bookcase.

You don't realize how loud paper is until you unfold it in a room run by a librarian turned media specialist. I panic and scoot my chair up closer to the table. The metal tips of my chair's feet scrape against the tile and this is so noisy, it covers the paper-crinkle sound enough that I can unfold it and slide it under my binder. Unnoticed. The specialist lady looks up, but I'm far enough away now that she can't see me clearly.

I pull the note out in slow motion under the table, showing only the last few lines and working my way up from the bottom.

W is written all cursive-y and awesome at the signature part.

Wreni wrote about how her new house is so full of unpacked boxes, she still can't find some of her stuff, about how she's so excited to hang again and that her brother got grounded from the computer because he spilled orange juice all over the keyboard.

Because everyone has a cell phone with texting (except for me because I might as well be an Amish kid), I decide I should note her back right away. I unlock the three rings of my binder, take out a sheet of paper and pinch the rings closed. Plain pencil will have to do for my first one. I can't think of anything that isn't completely lame so I erase and rewrite a few times before settling on some yakety yak about Yoplait and how I was thinking about trying to make cookies as yummy as the Halloween ones her mom made. I finish it with, "I wonder if Horse Girl notices how much she looks like a horse today with that extra-tall ponytail." That'll make Wreni crack up. I fold the paper into fours and stuff it into the inside pocket of my Science binder. Safe and sound.

Mrs. Martin's in the doorway after the hour's up to gather everyone for Science and we shuffle back to our classroom. I sit behind a kid who always looks confused, with his mouth hanging open a little bit so you see the bottom of his front teeth at all times.

People are zooming to their seats and Mrs. Martin is already on someone's case about not being settled "at four minutes past nine o'clock, the official start of class."

Horse Girl is looking especially snooty-pants, sitting two seats ahead of me. When she turns around to collect the rest of the row's homework, she looks right at me for a second or two and flips her hair all girly-girl-ish and annoyed.

Everyone starts taking notes because Mrs. Martin says something like "this will be on the test."

Mrs. Martin wastes no time getting into her lecture. You never know if she'll fire out questions to make sure people have paid attention and didn't write notes to each other. Timing is everything.

I open my binder and pull out the note from the

side pocket in one smooth action, slipping by Mrs. Martin's radar eyes. I am sweating, so I take off my sweater, but it doesn't help.

Wreni is looking pretty bored, slumped down in her seat with her head propped up by her hand.

Get it over with, Easter.

Blocking out visions of Mrs. Martin catching me mid-passing, I tighten my fist around the note so you can't see any paper between my fingers. All in fast forward fashion.

I poke the kid in front of me who is doodling stickmen complete with cowboy hats and lassos. The eraser part of my pencil is probably too soft, because he doesn't turn around, so I poke again, this time with the corner of my assignment notebook.

"Psst."

He turns slowly, annoyed, like I'm interrupting him creating a masterpiece or something.

Lowering my head, I am eye level with his shoulder, blocking Mrs. Martin's view. Holy macaroni. I'm noting someone. "Pass this to Wrrrrennni, please," I mouth and nod my head toward the kid to his right in the desk behind Wreni. He stares for a second or two and I think about repeating it, but before I can, he grabs the note from my outstretched hand.

I say a speedy, silent Hail Mary and double check that Mrs. Martin still has her back to the class, drawing some alien-ish doo-dads that have something to do with thermal energy on the dry erase board.

Look back, Wreni. I wish I had some kind of telepathic power. She's zoned out, recreating Mrs. Martin's diagram as super cool pink and purple bubbles.

That's when I notice the kid tapping my note against Horse Girl's back.

"No, no, wrong person!" I whisper.

Too late.

Horse Girl is a pro, already unfolding it under her desk. You'd think she'd read the "Hey Wreni" at the top and pass it to her neighbor. But she doesn't.

Reading other people's notes. Just another reason why she's the worst. Then, that's when I see it in my head. At the bottom of the plain penciled note: the part about Horse Girl's ponytail. Since no other girl in our grade has a tall ponytail today, she'll know it's about her. I shut my eyes, fast, as if that will help.

Mother of all fudgsicles.

My stomach is topsy-turvy with twisty waves of nausea, and for a few seconds, I stop hearing. I go over the instant replay in my mind while I stare straight at Mrs. Martin's wrinkled eyes and moustache-y mouth. I half convince myself that I imagined the whole thing.

Flipping noodles. I never should have written that stupid note in the first place. I say twelve silent prayers in a row and imagine my guardian angel looking on, shaking her head in a tisk-tisk kind of way.

Horse Girl never looks back. Not even once.

Usually, she's flashing smiles at Tommy and bating her ogle eyes at her boy-obsession-of-the-week sitting somewhere near me.

She's planning her revenge. I can tell.

Mrs. Martin looks more intense than ever. She's really into this thermal energy stuff with her arms flailing all around. How can I focus on Science when total unpredictable chaos is looming? I get dizzy imagining Mrs. Martin screaming in my face, pointing to the note and patting Horse Girl's shoulder like she'd just been the victim of a hate crime.

Thing is, I don't even feel sorry for writing it. I mean, I feel sorry for her seeing it, but there's been a volcano brewing inside me for a while.

Wreni is sitting there, probably thinking I'm a total wuss for not writing her back.

I think about how Horse Girl will do something to make me look so ginormously stupid that Wreni won't want to be friends with me anymore anyway.

My mind is all knotted up and my stomach feels cloudy. I'm sweating cold and that awful, nauseating lump thing makes its way from my stomach up to my throat.

Escape routes form in my mind. I will run through the door and down the hall, past the main office and through the front door. Without notice.

I scan the room and feel pangs of jealousy that my classmates' biggest problem is staying awake through Mrs. Martin's lecture. My eyes hit Horse Girl. The note's gone and she's staring at the floor tiles. I watch for clues on her revenge. At the end of class, Horse Girl walks out while talking to another kid, but he seems a lot more into the conversation than her.

I avoid lingering in the hallway on account of knowing that Horse Girl is always hanging around, so I head to the restroom and pick the first stall. That's when I hear her boots slam down against the grimy tile and stop at the mirror. I forgot she makes frequent stops here to smooth out her ponytail and apply lip gloss that smells like tropical fruit. Her boots are well down the hallway when I finally head to Language Arts.

Without looking at anyone, I settle into my seat near the front.

Be brave, Easter.

My seat feels slippery against my skirt and for a second, I think about letting my body slip right under the desk and crawl to the door.

When I finally look up, Horse Girl drops her backpack to the floor and LOOKS BACK AT ME.

I freeze, unable to look away, and await a mouthed threat or cuss or public humiliation bad enough to run me out of town.

But she just stares, not glaring or frowning or smirking or flashing a 'you're-so-gonna-regret-messing-with-me' look. Not knowing her reaction makes it about a gallizion times worse, of course.

It's impossible to concentrate when you have zero

clue what is going to happen and you know for a fact nothing good is going to come.

• • • TEN

There's really nothing worse than telling your whole body that it's time to go to sleep when it's totally aware of the situation. No fooling it.

Sleep tonight is impossible, on account of everything in my life whirring around out of control.

Horse Girl's going to ruin Operation Cool. Mom is getting worse. I can't guess what's next.

Normally, I'd be all right with only telling Yoplait all about it. The fact is she's a good listener but I need advice. From a real person. I can't call Grandma Dottie because it's obvious what would happen. She'd get upset and drive here in a rush. Mom would scream and yell. Dad would find out how bad Mom's drinking has become. Grandma would cry. Dad would divorce Mom. Mom would never speak to Grandma Dottie again. Not like they're talking now anyway, but it would be worse.

Yoplait's acting weird, walking around my room like she just can't find a decent spot to sleep. I've read that cats can sense when a thunderstorm is coming. They act all nervous and start pacing around. Thing is, I haven't heard of anything stormy in the forecast.

I get up.

Dad's in the living room watching sports broadcasters argue about stuff.

"Hi, Dad."

"Hi. It's late, Easter," he says without looking at me.

Talk to him.

"Can't sleep?" He lifts one eyebrow up.

"Nope."

"A glass of milk will help."

I stand there for a few seconds, hoping for a burst of courage.

"Um, Dad?"

"Yes." The people on the TV are in a shouting match.

"Can I just sit here for a few minutes?" I walk over to the couch and sit down before he responds. Amigo trots and lays down right over my feet. Normally, I'd think he didn't want to miss anything fun but this time, I think he's there to make me feel braver.

Dad lowers the volume on the TV.

"Sure, Easter," he says, with a hint of worry. "Everything okay?"

"Yep, just not tired, I guess." I lean down and pet Amigo.

"It's important to get enough rest, Easter."

I want to say, "Really? Rest? Maybe you should rest. You're never even home." I'm silent instead.

He's a lot like this house with blinds closed all of the time.

"Do grownups go through phases?" I ask in my best grownup tone, and pausing between each word.

He looks at me for a few seconds and then back at the TV, then up to the ceiling like a million things are running around in his mind.

"I suppose, Easter," he says softly. "Where is this coming from? Something related to Mom?" He sets the remote beside him and leans forward. "Are you worried about Mom? Did something happen today?"

Amigo's fur grows itchy against my feet so I pull them up and swing them around and fold them under me.

"No, no, I was just wondering." Inside, my stomach does a summersault and I add, "You know, because kids at school go through phases, at least that's what the teachers always say. I wonder if it's part of being a grownup, too." I twist the bottom of my shirt.

"Hmm, Easter, I think you should just focus on being a seventh grader and not worry about being a grownup. You're only just a girl!" He smiles, like 'be a good kid and go get your rest.'

"Yep," I say in my most convincing voice.

The commercial break's over on TV so he raises the volume again. It's my cue.

"Night, Dad."

"Goodnight, Easter."

Amigo follows me to my bedroom.

I dive onto my bed and bury my head into a giant pile of stuffed animals.

The strangest feeling ever comes over me. I'm like an astronaut floating in outer space, all un-balanced like when you're about to fall sleep and you dream that you trip over a curb and land in the middle of a busy street.

Yoplait is stretched out on her side, one paw under my closet door, which doesn't shut all of the way on account of its crackly painted hinges. The last time she'd been alone in the closet, I found her trying to swallow half a shoelace. I wave my hand up, like 'no-no.' She opens the door, anyway, in ten million creaky movements. When she finally makes the opening big enough to fit her head, she's upright in an instant, pushing her head between the wall and door. Creeaaaak. She scoots inside fast, as if the noise caught her off guard.

I wrap my fuzzy blanket around my shoulders and up to my chin until it's too itchy. From inside of the closet, there's a rustling and a soft uh-oh kind of meow. The door swings open and slams against the bookcase. Yoplait flies out, tail first. Amigo barks but stays seated on the other side of the room.

Before I can say "whoa," Yoplait is on the bed, pawing the blanket for an opening until she successfully makes a tent big enough for her head and scoots in.

That's when I see a tiny photo album on the floor, beneath the Encyclopedia of Dreams I'd bought at a library sale, among shoeboxes and scattered notebooks. I get out of bed and thumb through the pages. They're all photos of when I was a baby and a toddler and a preschooler and a third grader. When things were normal.

Heartbreaking sunflowers.

I think about ripping it up into tiny shreds but I throw it back into the closet instead.

Face it. Mom's getting worse, Easter. I've been completely, utterly, pathetically, overly optimistic about the whole thing. Her being back to normal is light years away, if possible at all on account of everything that's happened. Mom is off on another planet when she's drinking. It's like watching her hurt herself inside a glass room, but without a way for me to get in and help her. The more I think about it, the more I realize that Dad isn't around much at all anymore, either.

What-ifs swirl and eat up my insides and grow, especially when I think about the whole Horse Girl situation. I imagine Horse Girl punching me and my face becoming all messed up like an old-time boxer.

She'll beef up her daily insults and teasing. That's how revenge goes, because I threw a fist full of dynamite on the whole thing.

Then there's Wreni, who'd probably think it was pretty uncool of me to write that mean stuff about Horse Girl anyway. If she finds out, she'll think I'm the kind of person who goes around writing bad stuff about everyone.

I could play sick and skip school tomorrow but of course, of all days, I have a math test.

My insides crush together and I cry the silent kind of sob with my face pressed between a stuffed unicorn and a scratchy-fur grey penguin.

But it feels good, like the tears are washing away a big thick pile of mud and gunk that has been forming inside me for a while.

I shiver and wipe a few drops of sweat from my forehead.

At five twenty two a.m., the garage door closes and I listen to the gravel crinkle under Dad's truck tires.

Amigo stands and stretches his back legs and then his front and then shakes his whole body, as if he'd just gone for a swim. Maybe he did in his dream!

He looks at me with his best hungry-dog face. He knows I won't go back to sleep now.

In the kitchen, I fill his bowl with food and it overflows a little. As I'm picking up those extra pieces, I hear the staircase creaking.

"Mom?"

"Yes," she says when she appears in the kitchen.

"What are you doing up so early?"

"Couldn't sleep," she says to the coffeemaker as she turns it on.

"Me either."

"How about French Toast?" She smiles!

"Really?" I know it probably sounds stupid but the idea of having Mom's French Toast for the first time in a long while is marvelously exciting.

"Go on back to sleep for a while and I'll call you when it's ready," she says while picking out her favorite coffee mug from the cabinet.

"Okay," I say and head to my room.

I listen to clang clanging for a few minutes and I picture Mom setting out the mixing bowl, a giant spoon, a pan and all of the ingredients. I wait for the yummy aroma to arrive in my room.

After ten minutes of brushing Yoplait's fur and bribing her with treats all the while, I decide that I should check on Mom because it's weird that there's no sound coming from the kitchen.

I find the ingredients and the cooking stuff out, as I pictured, but there's no Mom. I notice that there are no eggs out so I check the refrigerator. No eggs.

She probably gave up since she's missing a main ingredient.

On the deck, I find her, asleep.

I don't eat any breakfast because I'm not the tiniest

bit hungry anymore anyway.

When I arrive at school, my brain is a bit foggy from hardly any sleep. I settle into my seat with a wave at Connor and a smile at Wreni.

Part of me wants to see Horse Girl strut in and make a remark about how weird my thrift-store sweatshirt is. Just to get whatever's coming over with.

But she never comes.

We're half way through math when Mrs. Martin gives us a five-minute break while she checks her email or something.

I sign out the bathroom pass in the back of the classroom and when I get to the door, Tommy Hansen opens it for me and whispers, "Hold on, one sec" with a smirk.

My "thanks, okay" is delayed as I watch him sign out the other pass. With a couple of quick strides, he meets me in the doorway again and closes the door behind us.

"Hey." He doesn't walk away.

"Hi."

"Listen, I'm having some people over tonight. Just to hang out, you know."

A wobbly "uh" flies out.

"You should really come. It's people from seventh grade and maybe a few eighth graders 'cause they're on my baseball team."

"Oh, um, yeah, thanks for the invite."

"Wreni. You're friends with her, right?"

"Wreni? Yeah."

"You can bring her, too, if you want."

One of the office ladies takes a few steps at the end of the hall and says, "Get moving, kids. Where are you supposed to be?"

"Oh sorry!" I shout and we head toward the bathrooms and the office lady disappears down another hallway.

"So, everyone's coming over around six so whenever you want to drop by. Do you know where I live?"

"Yeah, across the street at Brushell in the yellow house on the corner," I say, far too quickly. Yeeesh.

"Awesome," he says.

"I'm not sure I can make it," I say.

"It's okay. If you can, cool. If not, still cool."

Holy, holy.

• • • ELEVEN

There's an old time movie playing on the TV in the living room that wakes me before the alarm has a chance to blare. I can tell it's old by the way people talk to each other and the jazzy song playing in the background.

My bed squeaks when I swing my legs around and stand.

On my dresser is a chocolate chip cookie in a little bag next to a blue note card that's prettifed with a giant, hand-drawn red heart. Inside it reads, "Easter Ann, I'm sorry about the French Toast. Love you, Mom."

I tiptoe from my room, avoiding the creaky parts. Mom's curled up and snoring on the couch. It's been a while since she's watched movies. It feels good and normal because we used to watch those old movies and sitcoms together, with Grandma Dottie. Those movies and shows make life in the 1950s and 1960s seem so simple and good. People didn't go around having to pretend nothing's out of whack. Problems were solved in thirty minutes or less.

In the kitchen, I'm really surprised to find Dad. He's been leaving extra early for work. But this morning, he's at the kitchen counter reading a newspaper. He buys a printed copy sometimes. Like I said, he's not a fan of the Internet. Before, Mom had always scrubbed off the smeared newspaper ink from the white counter. Now there are gray smudges everywhere. Mental note: Take care of that.

"Morning, Giggles," he says. It's been a while since he's called me that.

"Morning, Daddio," I say because that's what I used to call him.

I slurp half a glass of orange juice to make my throat feel all refreshed. When I was little, I called it a "glass of sunshine."

Next, I stand at the pantry, mentally debating whether Cinnamon Toast Crunch is better than Honey Nut Cheerios. I decide on Cheerios, fill a bowl, squeeze the bear-shaped honey bottle and drizzle a smiley face over the top. Some of the honey sinks so it's an extra treat as I near the bottom.

"Something about that bear shape makes the honey taste sweeter," I announce to Dad. He peeks from behind the Sports section and smiles.

It's nice to see Dad here and I am glad to have someone to eat breakfast with.

"Seems like your mother is extra tired this morning," he says and puts down the newspaper.

Silence.

"Hmm." I shovel in a mound of Cheerios.

He nods and says, "Got the morning off."

"Cool beans." He's checking up on Mom. While I'm noticing that it's not marked on the calendar, the phone rings and the caller ID says it's Grandma Dottie. I decide to answer because Dad's here.

"Grandma Dottie!"

"Oh, Easter dear, how's my darling granddaughter?" She's grinning, I can tell, and so am I. "How's seventh grade going?"

I just want to hug her in person. Grandma Dottie is classy hip and she never thought to adopt the old lady tight-curl perm or polyester pants. She shines goodness. You can tell when you meet her. On a single outing to the mall, Grandma will smile at a grumpy sales person or wave at a whining, beyond bratty kid— exactly the kinds of people you don't go out of your way to talk to. Grandma speaks and ta da! They're so much sunnier! And it's not be-nice-to-old-ladies fakeness, I swear.

"Well, lots of developments." I go to my room so I don't have to whisper on account of Mom sleeping on the couch. I fold my comforter over and Yoplait yawns. When I turn on the lamp, she flops a paw across her face. Nothing could be cuter.

I tell her all about Halloween with Wreni Hammer, Horse Girl being the worst, the Scoops incident, the Tommy Hansen moments and that Connor is actually kind of a friend now, too, I guess.

When I'm done, she says, "You just keep being yourself, okay, honey? Wreni sees how special you are and I'm sure you'll quickly become good friends with her. Be careful with that Tommy Hansen. Besides, who needs Tommy when you have Connor chasing after you?"

"No, uuuh no," I say, shocked. "It's not like that at all. Connor's just a buddy. A nice guy, dorky buddy."

"Uh huuhhh." She can be a real smartypants in a funny way. "Sounds to me like he's extra nice to you, dear."

"Oh Grandma, Grandma, Grandma," I say and sigh. "Don't be silly."

I want to tell her about Mom with all of my heart but I can't.

Yoplait sneezes a few inches from my face as I kneel beside my bed.

I'm thinking of my long-sleeved shirt with ruffles at the collar and my heart locket. I go right to my closet and slide on the special outfit that my brain woke obsessing over.

Left side. Right side. Over my shoulder, I check in the mirror. Yep, looks good. I feel good. I feel like me.

I pull my jeans up over my toothpick legs and it fits just right—no belt needed!

Okay, Easter, you're wearing this.

Then I write on the Status page of Operation Cool: "Wearing Me clothes today. Dancing walruses! Yeah! Woot woot!"

Before there's a chance for mind changing, I run down the stairs, feed Amigo and Yoplait and load the dishwasher.

I stick a yellow note on the sliding glass door handle that reads, "Careful, remember Yoplait! Love you! -Easter."

Dad drives me to school and while we're driving, I say ten prayers that Mom behaves.

"Have a great day, honey!" he shouts when I jump out.

At school, my clothes are a non-topic of talk on account of some kid's hockey injury that had him hobbling around with a crutch.

That is until Connor says at the start of Language Arts, "Sweet shirt, Easter!"

Heads turn.

"Ha, thanks." Stupid Connor. I search for a topic changer.

"Your mom let you dress all mismatched like that?" asks Brian, a pimply kid whose thing is playing the guitar but is a total nose picker when he's not making music.

"It's not mismatched," I say upbeat.

"Yeah, it is," he says and drums two pencils against his desktop.

"It's unique. I like unique things. Life's not perfect. Sometimes mismatched stuff is awesome."

That's when Wreni chimes in. "Yeah, Brian, you've got a unique look, too. It's called Just Rolled Out of Bed."

"Hey man," he says and laughs. "I like my wrinkled shirts."

The second I step off of the bus, I see Dad raking leaves beside our giant Maple tree out front.

Is he outside because Mom's in bad shape inside? Is he raking to busy himself because he doesn't want to be around Mom?

Dad waves. I'm still three houses away when I see Mom raking, too, near the other tree.

Yay! Yay! Yay! I run home and write on the Operation Cool Status page, "And just like that, things are falling into place!"

• • • TWELVE

There are three things I know about giant kitchen appliances: One. They help you make all kinds of yummy and not-so-yummy food, depending on what kind of cook you are. Two. They get hot. Super hot. Three. Never, ever leave something cooking and walk away for more than a few seconds.

If your mind's all cloudy, though, it's hard to remember these things.

A few weeks after the good yard leaf-raking day, I'm washing my hands in the bathroom after school when Mom announces out of nowhere, "I'm making spaghetti!" There's so much upbeatness in the way she says it that I almost don't believe it's her voice at all.

I push the faucet handle back at snail's pace and listen for more.

"Easter?" Mom calls from the other side of the

bathroom door.

"Oh, yes, okay, Mom."

Warm fuzzies hit my heart. Spaghetti never sounded so good.

I dry my hands as fast as I can with the little blue towel I always like because it has a furry rabbit at the bottom, then flip off the light and take two hops into the hallway.

Amigo, sprawled across the living room floor, lifts both eyelids, wags his tail and rolls over onto his back, like 'Belly rub, please!'

So I change course, kneel beside him and run my hand over his belly.

"You're a good boy, a really good boy!" I whisper. "Remember, age is only a state of mind, old boy!" That's what Grandma Dottie says.

Boiling water has a unique sound. It reminds me of being little. Mom was always making noodles, like every other day to be exact. I loved pasta more than anything.

There's clinging and clanging in the spatula drawer, then a long sigh and a curse and then, "Where's my noodle spoon?"

I know it's in the back, under the soup ladle and next to the ice cream scooper, but I don't say a word because she might be embarrassed that I know and she doesn't.

Cling. Clang.

"Finally!" she whispers. The drawer rolls back and

slams against the cabinet.

Mmmow. Yoplait meows from top of the stairs like what's all the noise about.

I tap my hand on my thigh twice and Yoplait trots down, belly swaying back and forth and sits next to me. I pet under her chin and on Amigo's head until I wonder if maybe Mom's up for talking.

So I plop on the counter stool, rest my elbows on the counter's grey smudges and place my face on my palms.

Mom opens the long plastic sleeve of spaghetti sticks and it rips down the side, letting more than a few sticks escape and fall to the floor before she grips the sleeve.

So I jump off the stool, pick up the sticks, twirl to the garbage can, press the swinging lid and toss them in.

"Thanks," Mom mumbles and sets the sleeve on the counter beside the noodle scooper. "You have homework?"

"Yes," I say, surprised. "Always, usually."

"Well, you better get on that," she says semi-stern.

Most of my homework is already done but I don't tell her that. I just say, "Yeppers," because it feels good to be reminded of normal things like that.

I'm sitting on my carpet, noticing that it's covered with a lot of fur and little fuzz balls that fall off my socks because it's been too long since I vacuumed. It's just so heavy to lug up the stairs. I'm thinking about running it when Amigo opens my door by banging it against the wall, dropping his favorite blue rubber ball at my feet.

"Playful today, eh?"

"Ruff!" He tosses his head back to the door and backs up three feet.

"Okay." I get on my knees, grab the ball and follow him down the hallway, to the stairs, out the door to the front yard.

"Rooooo!" Amigo sings when I toss the ball across the grass.

His legs don't move all that fast anymore but by the looks of his tail, he's loving it.

When he catches the ball and drops it on my bare feet, the corners of his mouth push way up high. Seeing a smiling dog is good for a person, like peppermint ice cream and sunsets.

"Here it comes, Amigo, up up!" I cradle the ball in my hand, wind my arm back like a professional shotput star, and spin on my feet.

Amigo leaps, catches it mid-air and takes a victory lap sprint around the yard.

"And he's got it, people!" I shout sportscaster style. "That's it, Amigo! Yeah yeah yeah! And the crowd goes wild. Woo woo!"

In the middle of the lawn, I meet Amigo and lift his front legs up to rest on my shoulders. "Good job, champ!"

"Roo!" He says, like 'Thanks.'

That's when I catch poor Yoplait sitting on the living room windowsill, ticked off with silent bellowing meows and a whipping tail.

I wave, toss a kiss in the air and promise to be in soon. Amigo snatches the ball and takes off, looking behind, like 'Chase me!'

In these moments, where he has bursts of energy, you can really tell his papa was a German Shepherd. When I catch him and grab the ball, he jumps up and licks my face. That comes from his mama being a sweetheart Golden Retriever.

"Okay, two more throws and then we'll go in so Yoplait doesn't hide your toys out of jealousy again," I say and glance back at the window.

This time, Yoplait's not in pout mode. Instead, she's pacing back and forth on the sill and meowing long ones. I can tell because her mouth hangs open a while before closing.

"Yoplait! You big baby!" I shout and throw the ball for Amigo.

But she's not okay with it. She leans on her back paws, steadying herself as the weight settles to her butt, presses her belly to the glass and places her front paws on the glass high above her head.

"Yoplait!"

She stares right into my eyes and her tail is stiff.

"Yeeesh! Okay!"

Amigo follows me and when we're barely through the front door, says, "Ruff, ruff, ruff!" Each bark is louder and faster than the other. He charges past me and into the kitchen.

"What's wrong?!" I sprint behind him.

I make it to the kitchen in three hops. Smoke clouds hover over the stove and there's a snake-y snizzle coming from the pot.

The pot of water for the spaghetti!

"Oh no! Oh no! Oh no!"

Amigo zigzags across the kitchen.

"Ruff ruff ruff!"

"I know!" I shout.

I scan the room but there's no towel around.

Mom must have moved it.

And then…beeeeeeeeeeep!

The smoke detector. Great.

Yoplait runs for the cover of the living room and Amigo follows.

I find two towels in the laundry room and fold them across my hands. Then I grab the handles and pull up.

What do I do with it?

"Mom! Mom!" There's panic in my voice. It's loud and shaky. No response.

Into the sink the pot goes with a thud.

I bat at clouds of smoke and turn the stove knob to the off position and flip on the fan.

In the closet, I find a broomstick and because I once saw Grandma Dottie do it, I stab the button on the smoke detector with the end of it.

The beeping stops.

Unable to breathe without coughing, I run to the living room to check on Yoplait and Amigo.

I open the sliding glass door but leave the screen in place.

I slam my hand against the screen and the frame of it vibrates against the glass.

Still, this doesn't wake Mom. She's deep in sleep.

Yoplait blinks, like 'I know, Easter, I know.'

Just try to be friendly.

"I like your boots."

It's all I can think to say when the math teacher announces that we have a group project and directs Horse Girl to take the seat next to me. Out of thirty kids. Really, lady? This is it. She's going to take me down.

Horse Girl's boots are leather, tall and actually kind of cowgirl Annie Oakley-ish. They go well with her faded skinny jeans, if you're into that style.

"Thanks," she mumbles after a did-you-really-just-try-to-compliment-me glare. Then she laughs. Hard! She whispers something to the girl behind her and doesn't even make a hand shield over her mouth!

I think about Operation Cool. Things are going well. Things will keep going well. I still use that fake confidence trick Grandma Dottie taught me.

My tongue turns desert-y again and I am sweating cold.

That's when it happens.

"Easter, what's up with your mom," Rachel says sharply, hitting my ears like daggers. She taps her desk with magenta nails and continues, not waiting for a response. "What's her deal?" Her mouth hangs open a little. Some of the kids are listening; I can tell because it gets a little quieter around us.

"What?" I swallow and it echoes. I move my pencil into the crease of the book.

"My mom tried to make friends with her this summer," she says, twirling the end of her hair around her fingers. "She saw her at the grocery store a few times. My mom said she feels sorry for her because she doesn't seem to know many people around town so she invited her for coffee and barbecues and other stuff but your mom said, 'Oh thanks but I'm busy' every time."

I shift in my seat and scan the tiles on the floor. "Oh, she is busy working on the house." I giggle for effect. "You know, summer projects and stuff." I wonder why the heat is on so high because I'm super warm.

"That's totally bizarre-o." Her eyes are fixed on me, analyzing my response. I flush and fidget with the bottom edge of my shirt. When I get the guts to look up, she smirks in a way that hurts.

Horse Girl chimes in. "My grandpa said she never goes anywhere."

No funny, smooth response pops into my head so I

just shrug my shoulders, spin around and as if on miraculous cue, the math teacher tells the class to turn to a certain page of our textbook.

Rachel whispers to Horse Girl, "My mom said she was always buying wine and beer."

My stomach flips.

Please, please stop. Let Wreni not have heard that. Instant replay of the whole conversation repeats in my mind so it's a while before my face finally cools.

As I'm packing up my backpack, Wreni taps me on the shoulder and squats next to me.

She whispers, "Hey, what was all that about your mom today? Is she okay?"

I pretend to be ultra-busy getting my math folder to fit between a couple of books.

"Oh, you know how it goes," I say. "They make up stuff." My face burns. I'm so sorry for lying.

"Yeah, that's what I figured," Wreni says in an upbeat way. "Just making sure."

"Ha, yeah, of course," I say, zipping up my bag.

"But was it true?" She stares. "I mean about what Rachel said about her mom trying to make friends with her?"

My "I dunno" comes out short and sharp and I feel bad right away when I shut my locker with a bang.

I don't feel like smiling or talking. I just want to zap myself home. It's probably pretty clear by my face because Wreni doesn't say much more, except the usual "see ya tomorrow" and goodbye wave when I'm a few feet from my bus.

••• THIRTEEN

Dad, Yoplait, Amigo and I watch Detroit's Thanksgiving Day parade on TV. All four of us fit on the couch. It feels good like it did when I was a kid. We even eat the strawberry pancakes Dad made, right there on the couch—with syrup and all!

All the while, there's a cloud hanging above. I'm thinking about how Mom's signature Thanksgiving dish is mashed potatoes but it's ten in the morning and she is still sleeping. I'm wondering at what point Dad will shout, "Sue! Get up! Half the day is nearly gone!"

Just as the ginormous Clifford passes through rows of skyscrapers, Dad says, "Your mom should be awake by now. We told Grandma that we'd be there in the early afternoon."

Like no big deal, I say, "Okay, I'll wake her." I scoot Amigo with one foot so I have room to pass.

The coffee's brewed already so I stop in the kitchen, pretend to be washing syrup from my hands but I'm only running water to cover the sound of pouring a mug full of coffee and adding a drop of creamer. Dad would say, "Mom can get up and pour her own coffee," if he knew.

I tiptoe from the kitchen without catching Dad's eye and start up the stairs holding the mug with both hands, ever so careful not to freckle the cream carpet.

"Yoplait, stay," I mouth. Last thing I need is to trip over her while she's trying to beat me to the landing.

When I knock on their bedroom door, Mom doesn't respond so I open the door by turning the knob ultra slowly and pressing my toes against the bottom.

"Happy Thanksgiving, Mom!" There's no response so I repeat it, louder this time.

She scrunches her face and slides upright. "What time is it?"

"After ten."

She rubs sleepiness from her face.

"I brought you coffee."

For the first time in a long while, she smiles and takes the mug from me.

I smooth out a spot on the comforter and sit down. It's silent but we have a short moment where it feels kinda normal. For a second.

Dad makes the promised mashed potatoes because Mom takes forever getting ready. The two-hour ride to Grandma Dottie's house is long and quiet, though I ramble a few times about school and this and that.

When we pull up to the house, Grandma Dottie's front door opens and she steps out, waving so big, I worry she'll fall over.

All is fine at dinner until Mom goes out to have a cigarette on the back porch.

I'm at the little kids' table, pretending to be totally into my cousin's unbearably boring story about his skateboarding stunts.

At the table with the grownups, I hear Dad lower his voice, which only alerts my ears even more. "She's still good with Easter but, I just," he says and sighs, "I think she's really—"

My cousin raises his voice and moves his arms around for effect. I shred the corners of my napkin in my lap.

••• FOURTEEN

"Hey, what's up?" Connor whispers in my ear as we line up for Advisory. "How's your photography?"

Why's he always asking about that?

"Ah, okay," I turn my head and whisper over my shoulder. "I haven't done much lately. Just Lake of Eileen in the fall a bit."

"Sweet!"

"I guess it's really not that important for me, especially now that it's cold out." Maybe he'll quit asking about it, if I dull it up.

"What?" He asks loud enough to make the kid in front of me turn around. "You gotta keep doing what you love. It's good for ya."

"Yep." I stare at the back of the kid's head in front of me.

"You, my friend, are a victim of disorganized

thinking," he says in a hushed, weird voice.

"Movie quote?" I whisper.

"Yep. Wizard of Oz. 1939."

"Ahh."

"You know one reason I like movies, Easter?" Connor asks without waiting for a response. "It's like for just a bit, I don't have to think about the messed-up crap in my life. I can pay attention to someone else's story. I bet photography's like that, for some people."

With that, the line moves forward.

On my way to my locker at the end of the day, Connor pulls on my sleeve, even though I already see that he's next to me.

"There's this book," he says without a hey or whatever. Did I just hear him swallow? "You don't need it or anything because you're already good but I found this book about photography and stuff and I thought you would, I dunno, want to look at it, and keep it." He stops right in the middle of traffic to dig through his backpack and two seventh graders glance at me like 'get out of the way.' I shuffle a little to the side so that we're not both blocking traffic.

He hands me a tall book with glossy photos of incredible landscape and city photos arranged in an interesting pattern on the cover.

"Oh, oh." What the heck? He's giving me a book? "Where'd you get it?" I flip the book over and over in my hands like it's a shiny rock or something because I don't know what else to do.

"It's one of the many things my dad planned to do but never did." Connor says, staring down the hallway and gripping one of the straps of his backpack. "He's good at photography, but he spent his time on other stuff."

I nod because what do you say to that?

"You're good at it," he says and tugs on the strings of his hooded sweatshirt. "If you like it, you should shoot more. Do what's fun for you. For YOU. Maybe photography can remind us of all that once was good and that could be again."

"Yeah."

"That last one was from Field of Dreams. 1989, in case you wondered."

"Got it."

"Just don't go getting a big head, Ansel Adams."

"Who?"

"Man, you really need to read that book!"

Jake, another kid in our class, pretends to punch Connor in the gut as he passes, so he turns and heads to his locker.

I remind myself to keep walking.

• • • FIFTEEN

I button my jacket all the way up and stuff my hands deep into my pockets after the bus drops me off at home.

The air is extra stingy. Yoplait doesn't like the super cold so that's good with me. She won't want to dash outside as much and chase whatever animal happens to cross her turf. That door to summer adventures doesn't exist in the icy winter. Problem is, she hasn't realized this yet.

When I get in, Mom's at the counter with tomato soup and crackers.

She's awake. She's eating!

"Hey, Mom!"

"Hi, Easter."

"How are ya?"

Pause. "Fine. You?"

"Well, at school today, this kid Jeremy Panicci, he's real good at the piano but kind of knows it. Anyway, he played a song he wrote himself. It was cool."

Mom gets up, rinses her bowl and spoon, and leaves them in the sink on account of the dishwasher still being full of clean dishes.

When I begin to put away the clean dishes, she mumbles, "I'll do that later, Easter," but I'm already doing it.

A minute later, Mom, bundled in her winter coat, boots and no mittens (you can't hold a cigarette with mittens on), unlocks the sliding glass door.

Cling clang. I put a dish on the shelf a lot less gently than I should. I load her tomato-rimmed bowl on the top rack of the dishwasher.

As Mom opens the door, a peach-and-white fur blur appears in the corner of my eye.

Clang! I drop the spoon and it hits the steel sink.

Yoplait jumps at the sound and Mom slides the door closed in the nick of time.

Close one. Again!

While I'm there, near the door, I notice that it's snowing! First fall of the year. Ginormous flakes float like bubbles and prettify the air but melt when they hit the ground.

Photo shoot time.

I bundle up, wrap my camera strap around my arm, slide my feet into boots and stand in the middle of the driveway, letting the snowflakes polka dot my face. It's dark so I adjust the settings on my camera and photograph in every direction.

Like Connor said, it really makes me feel good, for reasons I can't name.

• • • SIXTEEN

The only thing good about decorating a Christmas tree by yourself is that you can put all of your favorite ornaments front and center. Naturally, mine are all from Grandma Dottie—featuring angels, Santa hat-wearing puppies and skiing elves.

I'm jamming to Jingle Bell Rock on my MP3 player and shimmying from the box of ornaments back to the tree when I happen to glance back at Yoplait atop the couch and notice that she's in attack mode with a puffed-up tail.

"Yoplait! No!"

Too late. She attacks a swaying ornament at high speed. I put my arms out to catch the falling tree but it's too heavy so I go down with it. Yoplait darts upstairs to wake Mom, I'm sure, and Amigo barks as fake tree needles rain over him.

Mom stomps on the floor in her room just above us and from the top of the stairs, she shouts, "What the heck is going on?!"

I'm inching my way from under the fat tree so I can't really respond.

"What are you doing, Easter?!" She's angrier this time.

Bad timing. The front door opens and Dad steps in, just as Mom yells, "You and that dumb cat!"

"Sue!" Dad drops three grocery bags beside the door and rushes over to pull the tree upright. "Help her!"

"She woke me up!" Mom says with a sharpness that's strong enough to even make Dad sad. I feel sorry for him. His shoulders slink back and he squats down to pick up the broken ornaments.

Mom stomps back to bed and the door shuts with a BAM!

We all look at each other like, 'Who is that woman?'

I'm petting Yoplait with I-know-it-was-an-accident extra sweetness and Dad puts all of the un-broken ornaments back on, but not the way I had them fixed.

"I brought home some cookies," Dad says. In the kitchen, he opens a package of green and red-sprinkled frosted cookies and pours two tall glasses of milk.

Between crunches, he asks, "Mom is not doing well today, eh?"

I twist my napkin. "Nope."

Amigo begs for a cookie but Dad reminds me that

cookies aren't good for dogs. I slide him one when Dad goes to "talk to Mom."

Dad heats two bowls of canned clam chowder for dinner but I'm not hungry because cookies before dinner means that all is not normal and that's not so appetizing. I just fold my laundry in my room.

••• SEVENTEEN

On the first official day of winter break, I still wake to my alarm clock set for a school day. Pressing the snooze button a couple of times without fear of being late is awesome.

I bundle up in my snow jacket and mittens and take Amigo out on his leash in the front yard to do his morning business because there's a layer of icy frost on the deck and old-man dogs are known to slip on that.

Yoplait watches from the living room window. Her tail whips like a windshield wiper.

With Dad already at work, I decide that today's a good day to work on Mom.

So I make a whole giant breakfast—scrambled eggs, toast and yogurt mixed with real strawberries. I pour extra coffee grounds to make Mom's coffee super strong. For extra niceness, on the tray, I put my frame that has my favorite photo of us.

At a snail's pace since Yoplait's my shadow, I carry the tray to her room. Figuring it's better to just drop it off and wait to talk to her until she's perked up, I whisper, "Hi, Mom. Here's your breakfast."

"Huh?" She rolls over to face me, eyes squinting from the hallway light.

"Here you go." I set the tray on the bed and walk out.

Just a few minutes later, Wreni calls!

"Hello?"

"Easter, hey!"

"Hey, Wreni." I play it cool.

"Happy Day One of Break."

"You, too!"

"Whatcha doin?"

I look down at the soapy sponge in my hand and the half smudge-free countertop. "Not much. You?"

"Bored already. My mom's making me go Christmas shopping with her."

"Oh, yeah?"

"Yeah, crowded mall equals zero fun. Unless..."

"Unless what?"

"Unlessss you wanted to go with us. Then it would be awesome."

"Oh!" I bite my lip and mentally debate whether working on Mom can wait until tomorrow and then I whisper, "I wish I could but I promised my mom that

I'd help with the house today. You know, decorate for Christmas and stuff." Forgive me for lying but the real reason is too...too not normal.

"Bummer."

"Yeah. Thank you, though. I mean it, it would have been great."

"Oh well. I'll just get dragged around the mall and wish you were there with me to laugh over how every store sells the same outfits."

"I'm sorry, Wreni. Really, I'd like to go."

"It's okay. You're lucky. Your mom probably already has her shopping done."

"Ha, yeah."

Operation Cool flashes in my mind and I shake it off. Things are on track. Missing one little thing won't slow me down.

"Well, have fun decorating, Easter."

"Thanks!"

"See ya!"

"See ya."

And that's it. I tell myself not to think too much about lying to her because it is only one more thing to worry about.

Mom comes down in her nightgown an hour later and rinses her dishes in the sink.

"Did you like it?" I smile my cutest from the table where I'm making cards for Grandma Dottie and others with construction paper and sparkly markers.

"Yes, thanks."

"Welcome. What do you want to do today? We could make cookies, OOOORRR," I say really excited like a game show prize announcer. "Even better, we could go out to eat and—"

"Nah, not today, Easter," she says and smoothes back her hair.

"Whyyy not," I say like a whiny kid at the toy store.

"Because."

I snap the top of my marker on and toss it at the table. It rolls and falls to the floor near Mom's feet.

She picks it up and hands it to me across the table without a word.

"Mom, pleeeeeeeeeze. Let's do something fun today."

"I'm not up for it."

That's when I lose it.

"You can't live like this forever!" I stand up, creating a gust of wind that scatters the cards and scraps of paper around the table.

"Excuse me?" Mom spins around. "Watch your tone, young lady!"

"Who are you anymore?" I slump back in my chair.

"I am fine," she says.

I watch her walk away to her own sad world again.

• • • EIGHTEEN

On Christmas morning, I wake Mom and Dad by sending Amigo in to say good morning with a lick on the face.

When Mom follows Dad out and they both say "Merry Christmas, Easter" at the same time, I nearly fall down the steps.

Even more jaw dropping, Mom and Dad make a big breakfast. TOGETHER. Mom, pancakes. Dad, omelets. What's extra awesome is that because it's Christmas, I get dessert at breakfast. Dad gives me half a glass of eggnog. It tastes like someone stuck a bakery in a blender. It's yummy but you sort of slip into a coma for a while afterwards.

After we open presents (I get a lot of books, a colorful painting of flowers for my bedroom wall and headbands but nothing related to photography), Mom excuses herself and says she's going to close her eyes for a bit.

Dad doesn't really question this much, as Amigo did wake them pretty darn early. But an hour before we're set to leave for church, Mom says she's not feeling well.

There's muffled shouting from behind their bedroom door.

"Sue! It's Christmas. This is ridiculous! And selfish!"

I don't know what Mom says back but it makes Dad even more ticked off. "Sue, you're ruining Christmas for everyone. Just like Thanksgiving. You're really great at putting yourself above your family!"

Packing up the presents under the tree, I hum Jingle Bells to drown it out. Mom, please. It's Jesus' birthday after all. Please.

At church, I sit between Grandma Dottie and Dad and stare at my favorite stained glass window—a guardian angel helping children safely cross a bridge. I close my eyes and say a prayer to God. "Please, please send an angel to help my mom. Please times a gazillion."

Just before the pies are cut and the cookie tins are opened at Aunt Deb's house, Grandma Dottie whispers and winks, "I'd like to chat with you for a minute, dear."

Worry hits my shoulders. It feels as real as if

someone dropped a couple of boulders on me.

I know she's just worried about Mom and five thousand questions will follow. I take a deep breath.

"Okay, Grandma," I say in my sweetest voice and follow her from the kids' table in the corner of the dining room.

My cousins are too busy trying to get a remote controlled helicopter to take off to care or even notice when we leave the room.

Grandma steadies herself with the handrail and links her other arm around my arm.

At the bottom of the steps, Grandma asks, "Easter, dear, is your mama all right? I mean, is everything okay with her?"

I stop one step from the bottom.

"Yeah, she's okay," I say as convincingly as I can. "She'll be more upbeat soon. You know, winter blues, I guess." If I don't lie, you'll worry.

Grandma nods. "You know you can call Grandma anytime you want. No matter the time. Okey dokey?"

"Yep, I know."

"Good. I've just been so worried. She won't answer when I call."

She wipes the worry from her face and pulls a box from behind the couch.

I wish I could tell you, Grandma. I wish I could. "Don't worry, Grandma. It's okay." I rub her shoulder.

"Now here. I don't want your cousins to see since I

didn't give them as much as I gave you but I want you to have this." She hands me a box tied with a purple ribbon.

I sit on the step and pull gently until the ribbon slips off and I lift the lid.

A zoom lens for my camera and a unique camera bag straight out of the 1970s with lots of color and personality!

I'm not embarrassed to admit that I break into a five-year-old's jump-up-and-down, excited dance.

"Oh thank you, Grandma! Thank you!" I wrap Grandma in a giant bear hug.

For a moment, it feels like Christmas did when I was little.

• • • NINETEEN

Updating Operation Cool seems like the thing to do at the start of the second half of the year but when I wake on the first day back to school, I don't know what to write.

With more snow and ice, Mom really won't leave. Now, she might not even go out to buy groceries. Without me home, will she drink more? What if she decides to cook again? What if I'm not here to make sure the house doesn't burn down? What if she forgets to let Amigo outside to do his business? What about Yoplait?

These what ifs are clouding up my head more than ever.

I'm in such a deep thinking zone, at school, I hardly wave when Wreni smiles at her locker.

In Advisory, I'm making note cards to study for our Science test when this stabs me in the ears and sinks my heart:

Megan says to Rachel, "My mom dragged me to the mall because she was on a last-minute shopping marathon and I ran into Wreni Hammer. We were both bored out of our minds so we hung out at the food court for a while. She's actually pretty nice when you get to know her."

Oh no!

"Seriously? She seems like she thinks she's better than everyone, to me," Rachel says.

"No, she's cool. I'm going to invite her to hang with us sometime."

I can't see it but I'm sure Rachel's face is squishing up.

"Really, you'll like her."

Great. That's it. I've lost my friend. There goes Operation Cool in a swooping gust of wind. Gone. Before I can stop it, tears layer my eyes and I stare at my note card. Don't blink. Tears will fall. After a few seconds, I have enough control of the tear situation to go up to the media specialist.

"I need to use the restroom, please," I whisper to her and stare at the countertop.

"Okay," she says with kindness so I know she can tell I'm about to break down.

I scribble my name on the hall pass sign-out sheet and close the door with a click.

The empty hall doesn't help keep the tears inside of my eyes.

I wipe them away and dry my hands on my jeans.

With the restroom to myself, I stand in a stall and hold toilet paper against my eyes.

I want to hate Wreni. I want to think that she's ditching me for the cool ones. I want to just give up.

But I know that it's not her. She asked me to go to the mall. I didn't go. It's not her fault that Megan was there.

Get a grip, get a grip!

When I've finally managed keep my eyes dry, I open the stall door just as Horse Girl's boots click through the door.

I sniffle like an idiot and take two big steps to the sink, pretending not to notice who exactly came in.

She pauses like she's watching me.

Shivering cubs. Please, please not now. She'll tell everyone I'm crying like a baby in here.

She slams her boot down on the tile and the sound bounces off the walls. I turn my hands over under the faucet stream.

Squeak.

The stall door swings open. To the door, I say, "I'm really sorry about that note."

I leave without drying my hands.

Part of me is relieved.

After lunch, we learn that there will be a Talent Show. I think the teachers just know that that there's nothing to do in March. Kids are bored.

It's common knowledge the only people who participate in the Talent Show are the kids with super interesting talents like jazz dancing and karate and guitar.

Mrs. Martin passes out the Signup to Participate Sheets. Four people in our class sign up immediately: a boy who's been taking karate since he could walk, the kid who can play the guitar and sing like a star but is a total nose picker when he's not making music, the son of a minor league baseball player who's super great at anything to do with running, throwing or catching; and Horse Girl, of course, she's doing a cheer.

Welp, I have no thing for a talent so there goes that.

Just before the dismissal bell, Mrs. Martin waves the signup sheet high in the air and clears her throat so loudly I swear the windows rattle.

"Tomorrow, I expect that we will have more students throw in their hats for this great opportunity to share your talents," she says, her face red in ticked-off mode. "Let us not be lackluster. I know there are a few in this room who are very talented."

Connor interrupts with a double sneeze from across the room. He flashes his dimples like he knows he just interrupted the lecture, and I smile back.

The bell rings and the class bunches out the door. I

lift my bag and swing it onto my back, knocking into someone.

"Whoa there!" Just Connor. Phew.

"Sorry!"

"It's all good," he whispers all laidback but then gets close to my face. Cue an unexpected butterfly-y feeling in my stomach. "Hey, are you going to do the Talent Show?"

"Hmm, I dunno." I'm thinking maybe it's a joke so I smirk. "Why?"

"I was just wondering," he says, as we walk toward the blacktop. "About your photos, I mean. You should show people your photography talent. You'd beat one of those schmucks."

Schmucks. I forgot how he talks grandpa-ish sometimes. That's sort of hilarious.

"I already told you that taking photos is not a cool talent, Connor," I say and roll my eyes.

"Are you kidding?" he asks before he cuts away toward his bus. "That takes more skill than cheerleading."

He grins real big before I turn away.

I'm almost out of earshot but I swear I hear my name.

"Huh?" When I swivel around, Connor's in the same spot, looking at me like he's about to say something and shuffling his foot against the loose dirt, but he takes off without another word.

He's kind of strange.

"Easter! There you are!" Wreni shouts and runs toward me like she's got some crazy awesome news.

"Hey!"

"Hey, I miss you!" Maybe the whole hanging-out-with-Megan thing was no big deal.

"Yeah, I know, me too!" I can't help but smile the kind that takes up my whole face.

"I've been dying to ask you something!"

"What's up? You win the lottery or something and you want to take me on a shopping spree in Chicago?"

"No! Pfff! I wish," she says. "Nah, I just wanted to tell you that we gotta do the Talent Show together!"

I take one step backward and shake my head. "Oh, I don't know about that."

"What?! C'mon, we'll do a duet and we'll dress all rockstar-ish!"

"Okay," I say and smile. "Tiny, minor, slight problem, though."

"Yeah! What's that?"

"I can't sing or dance."

"Get outta town. Sure you can! It's just karaoke. We'll practice. This will be our thing."

Our thing.

I picture it: Mom and Dad, front row, and Grandma Dottie, too. Plus Tommy Hansen, too, somewhere in the audience. Bright lights on the shiny stage. I lift my chin and spin around—ultra glam—with my vintage kitten-heeled pumps. The beat begins and Wreni and I dance in sync. The lyrics flow, smooth and silky, and the crowd's toes tap and heads bob. Mom and Dad whisper to all who'll listen, "That's our girl up there." Then Dad squeezes Mom's hand and whispers, "She's just like you," and they lean close and sway to the beat. They're the first to stand for an ovation that spurs whistles and clapping. Wreni and I exchange smiles, high five and curtsy. Then afterward, everyone crowds us. Tommy is there with a bunch of other kids but stops talking when Wreni and I walk in. Tommy comes up to me and says, "Man, you're awesome, Easter." I say ever so coolly, "As are you, Tommy." Then Wreni and I get invited to Scoops for a celebration with everyone. And Operation Cool is complete. And then...

Beep beep beep. The bus driver sends me back to reality and motions for me to get on the bus.

"Okay, we'll talk later, Wreni!"

"Okay!"

I'm in such a good mood when I get home, it doesn't even bother me that Mom's in bed again. I fill Yoplait's water bowl and add a couple of ice cubes because she really likes it extra cold. Amigo's food and water bowls are empty, too, so I fill them and after he finishes dinner, we play tug of war in the backyard. When we come back in, Yoplait follows me to my room. Cindy is always a bit of a showoff, swimming in and out of the castle house in the middle of her bowl. But Yoplait has no interest; she only watches with patience for my full attention again. That's the kind of thing you appreciate in a friend.

• • • TWENTY

It happens the very second I'm kneeling and unloading three books from my backpack into my locker.

I don't hear the knocking on my locker on account of the noise in the hallway between classes. It's when the door bumps my leg and I glance at the shoes next to me that I recognize the scuffmarks along the sides.

I'm still crouched like a mouse when I see his grin—the ear-to-ear kind—and a hi shakes from my lips.

"Hey," Tommy says. My legs cooperate and stand. I must be smiling because he says, "Whoa. Who is your dentist?"

Huh. My brain can't process the question. Must be a joke. Quick. Fake giggle. "Huhuhhu—"

"You had braces last year, right?" He runs his hand

across his chin. "I just noticed your smile is awesome. No, better than that. You have—" He checks out the ceiling and pauses for a second, and then he says, "A kickbutt smile."

I've never had a kickbutt anything so I'm on the verge of gushing over how I remember he got this green shirt for his birthday last year and that it makes him so look sixteen years old.

By the grace of Wreni, I snap out of it.

"Hey, Easter!" She's tugging on my sleeve and waving close to my face.

"Hi!"

"What's up, Wreni?" Tommy nods.

"Hey," she says and pauses while she loses her brain for a second, "Tom."

Silence. My jaw's hanging open and that's not very pretty so I remind myself to close it. Wreni's face is all, 'What? What I'd do?'

"I go by Tommy with everyone, actually." Tommy's mouth hangs open a little at first. Then he recovers from the surprise by running both hands through his hair though it's already smooth and perfect.

"Oh right." Wreni doesn't look sorry.

"No prob." Then he looks at me and says, "Talk to ya later."

I forget to respond.

"Peace, ladies."

"Bye, Tommy!" I say far too energetic.

"Adiós," Wreni says without looking.

I watch him as he disappears in the crowd.

"No way he keeps talking to us," I say. Maybe it's all meant to be this way. It makes a cute story, if you think about it. All of these years I've been secretly crushing and then now, maybe, he's tired of the other girls who've made it totally known they're into him for years. Maybe I'm different. And he likes that? Maybe that's it.

"What?" Wreni's baffled.

"Tommy," I say between deep breaths. "Just standing here, talking."

"Huh?"

She's new but I figure half a year is more than enough before it's clear: Tommy Hansen is the cutest by fifty yards and the coolest by a mile, which is exactly why there's a crowd of guys and girls surrounding him at all times.

"What is wrong with you," I say. "Tommy's the most popular kid in the whole school. Always has been."

"Yeah yeah." She scratches her forehead and lifts an eyebrow. "I don't get why. Bad news, if you ask me." Her school must have been full of Tommy Hansen-level guys. That or she hasn't been here long enough to get caught up in his crystal blue eyes.

"Those earrings!" I decide to change the subject when her earlobes sparkle in the fluorescent light. They're roses—silver and oh so unique.

"Like 'em?" Wreni grabs each ear.

"For sure!"

"My aunt was going to throw them out!"

"Nooo!"

"Yeah, seriously. I saved them!" She scans me for anything that remotely screams unique about my pink and grey-striped shirt and plain jeans. "So the talent show's like two weeks away already! We gotta get planning!"

"I know."

"Do you have any ideas about songs?"

"Whadya think of 'Girls Just Wanna Have Fun'?" I'm half expecting her to say she's never heard of it.

"Classic and perfect! I'll buy the karaoke version!" She claps her hands together. "Everyone loves that song! Ooh, ooh! And we can get fun outfits!"

"Yeah!" I think about Mom and how she'd totally know how to dress for it.

"Let's go shopping at that thrift store! Can I come to your house? My brother's totally annoying me lately."

"Oh, sure, I'll ask my mom." Worry, the extra heavy kind, lands on my shoulders like a thousand hundred-pound weights.

"Yay! How about next Friday?"

"Cool beans! Maybe we can go right from school" I force a giant smile.

"That sounds awesome!"

The hallway thins of people headed to class so we both say "see you later" at the exact same time like we've been friends forever.

When I get home, I interrupt Mom's TV watching. Maybe this is exactly how to get her out doing stuff. She'll love to help me with this!

"That's nice," she says without excitement. It's okay. She'll get into it when we start working on the song.

"So, that means you'll take us next Friday?"

"Yes, sure."

"Great, Mom! Thank you, thank you, thank you!" I throw my arms around her like I always used to. It feels good.

"Okay." She turns up the volume on the TV.

"Yoplait?" I skip across the living room to the stairs, when I realize that she hasn't come to see me yet.

From the top of the steps, I see the door to my bedroom open.

"Oooh no!" Cue major panic. "Yoplait!"

"If she's gone, if she's gone, if she's gone, I'll never forgive Mom," I say through gritted teeth. I check all of the places she could be including under my chair and in my closet.

Finally, I spot furriness in the corner of my eye. All but her head is covered by my white bedskirt.

"Thank goodness," I whisper. I kneel next to her so she climbs onto my lap and she doesn't mind when a few teardrops sprinkle her back. It is not fun to get so scared.

Maybe she's been scared, too.

For hours, I listen for Dad to get home and when I finally hear his truck in the driveway at quarter to ten, I tiptoe downstairs.

"Dad!"

"Hi, honey," he says while slipping off his shoes.

"I'm going to be in the talent show at school with Wreni!"

"Oh yeah?"

"Yes! We're singing a song!"

Uncovering the plastic from his plate of chicken and rice, he says, "I'm sure you'll have a great time doing that."

Back in bed, I write in Operation Cool: "Definitely found a best friend. Possibly found a thing to be known for, too."

••• TWENTY-ONE

At the meeting about the Talent Show after school, Mrs. Martin gives a big pep talk about how we're all so talented and yada yada—all meant to keep people from chickening out before show time.

Wreni and I head to the doors and from the shadow of the stacked chairs comes Tommy Hansen, in faded jeans and a tight brown t-shirt that makes his muscles stand out, mind you.

"Hey, I bet you guys will be awesome." He winks.

"Really? Thanks! We're just doing it to have fun." Pfft.

"Some of us are hanging out at my house for a little bit right now, since the meeting got out early. Wanna come?"

My legs turn to Jell-O.

"Ooh." I look at Wreni who's not a bit excited by

the invite.

"I live right—"

"Across the street. I know." I flush. "Yeah, maybe." Wreni shoots me an oh-puhleeeeze look.

"Sweet. Hopefully, we'll see ya both there." He bumps his chin in the air and winks as he passes.

"Seriously?" Wreni says.

"C'mon!"

"Okay, but only for a few minutes until my mom arrives."

"Yay!" I clap.

Tommy's mom answers the door. She's not very mom-ish. She's in a lot of a makeup and a sweater that shows part of her shoulders.

"Hi, girls," she says, and motions for Wreni and me to come in.

The house is nice and typical with a plaid couch and three identical lamps.

"Tommy," she calls. Bing. She picks up her cell and texts to someone while walking away into the kitchen.

There's running up the steps and then Tommy in an instant.

"You came! Come on down."

"Hi, yeah, hi!" My face burns.

"Hi, Wreni." He looks behind me.

"Hey," Wreni mumbles and stuffs her hands in her pockets.

I start to slide out of my flats with one foot against

the other but he says, "Nah, it's okay, Miss Manners." And he winks. Right at me. We follow him down the steps.

My pulse quickens.

Our shoes clickety clack against the tile stairs. I hang onto the handrail in case my legs give out on account of my horrible track record around Tommy.

The walls are made of dark wood panels and there are tons of posters of bands making growly faces.

I scan the room. There are a lot of eighth grade girls—mostly the snooty pants ones. They get quiet— for a second or two—but continue arguing over songs to add to Tommy's playlist.

We're all standing around in the backroom and Tommy says to a crew of eighth grade boys, "You guys know Easter Peters." He nods in my direction.

One of them says, "Yeah, Chief Maggie Mae's daughter, right?"

"Yeah." Tommy smirks. "And this is the new girl, Wreni."

"Hey," they say at the same time and look Wreni up and down.

"Hi," Wreni says, medium friendly.

Then down the steps comes Tommy's brother. He's taller than Tommy, with the same hair only shorter, but not so muscle-y. He must have been taking a nap or something because his hair looks like he hasn't been brushed in days and his jeans and t-shirt are all wrinkly.

A bad feeling seed forms in my belly.

"Whoa, invited the whole school?"

I didn't see it coming but right then, Tommy touches my arms and motions for Wreni and me to come to the area on the other side of the stairs.

Wreni shoots me a careful-there look and elbows me like 'let's get out of here.'

The baseball players head up the stairs and out the side door, leaving Wreni, Tommy and me alone.

"So, Wreni, I have a question for you," Tommy says softly.

"Okay," Wreni says with no eye contact.

"Do you wanna go for a walk or somethin' right now?"

I lean against the wall on account of my whole body being frozen.

Wreni grips my left arm and walks, pulling me behind her.

Tommy steps up close to her and looks right into her eyes so we can't move forward.

"Because I really think you're cool."

Wreni tugs but I don't move.

"Why don't you like give me a chance." He shrugs his shoulders back. "Easter thinks I'm cool." He steps closer and nods at me.

My face burns. My legs lock.

He likes Wreni. He never liked me at all.

Just Wreni.

"No, Tom, you're a real jerk!" Wreni screams and

stomps her heel onto his white sock-covered big toe.

"Ooooowwww!" He's mad like a little bratty kid whose toy got stolen by another kid.

Wreni shouts, "We're outta here!" and we run up the steps as if our lives depended on it.

From the front porch, we see Mrs. Hammer's minivan pull up at the school, ten minutes early just in case, and we dash at full speed across the street.

Mrs. Hammer jumps out of the car and if looks could kill, we'd be on the ground.

"WHAAT! Why did you just come from that house?!"

"I'm so sorry, Mrs. Hammer," I repeat three times in a row. "It's my fault! I should have known better than to go there. I'm sorry. It's not Wreni's fault."

After Wreni explains the whole story, Mrs. Hammer says, "Well, you girls definitely should not have gone without permission, but I appreciate the honesty."

"Also, Easter didn't know he's up to no good," Wreni adds. That's the kind of thing you appreciate.

Dad's truck pulls up next to the minivan and Wreni hugs me goodbye.

Mrs. Hammer doesn't tell Dad what happened and neither do I. How can I anyway? I'm fighting a major breakdown cry.

Dumb. Delusional. Doomed. I really am.

When we walk in the front door, Mom's on her way to the couch. By her walk, I can tell she's had a lot to drink.

"Sue!" Dad says. Then his face gets all authority figure-ish and he stands next to the couch preparing a major shouting lecture for Mom. I watch her settle into her usual spot there but I hardly recognize her. Her eyes are puffy and her hair looks like jumbled hay.

Waves of helplessness come over me. I am five years old again.

I want one of those mega phones to scream, "I can't take this!"

Right under my comforter I go, without even changing into my pajamas or anything. I fold my pillow and punch it as hard as I can. This causes a rush of tears. I'm too humiliated to hate Tommy Hansen. How insane was I to think he liked me? I don't know what's worse: Total crushing, humiliating pain that he never actually liked me at all? Or just disappointment that he's completely un-perfect on the inside and definitely not who I thought was exactly the guy for me? Or knowing that I got my new best friend caught up in the mess and ignored her warnings about him?

After a good, long sob, I open up Operation Cool and go nuts with my red pen. Where there's any Tommy this or that, I scribble red ink until it's like he was never a factor in Operation Cool at all.

This makes me happier, as stupid as that might sound.

Every time I use the phone at home, I fear the ultimate nightmare: Mom, in the background, all drunk and crazy acting while I'm trying to have a normal conversation with someone.

Wreni answers her cell phone with "Yaallow, sunshine!"

"Hey." I move the receiver away from my face so she can't hear my nervous swallow. "I just want to tell you I'm sorry about going to Tommy's."

"Don't sweat it!" She knows I've been crying. You can always tell a just-cried voice. "I was just about to call you, too! Do you want to rehearse tomorrow at your house?"

"I would love that but my mom has the flu." Guilt about lying wraps tightly around my whole body.

"Oh, you can come here then! My brother is going bowling with my dad. So we're annoying little brother-free!"

"Perfect."

In the basement, I find Dad in his chair across from his computer screen but he's only staring at the carpet near his slippers.

When I tell him about tomorrow's plan, he says, "That'll be a nice time, Easter."

I cannot believe how fast he OKs this.

• • • TWENTY-TWO

"Easter!" As we bunch out the door for lunch, Mrs. Martin scoots out her chair and motions me to her desk. She's holding up last week's Science homework. Since we were studying about how water freezes and stuff, I'd stapled a few print outs of the photo shoot I did at the lake in January.

"These are wonderful photographs of Lake of Eileen! Did you take them?"

"Yes." I nod.

"They are amazing! I'll give you ten extra credit points for being so thorough!"

"Thanks," I say and turn away as she writes seventy out of sixty points in red pen in the right corner.

I pray that no one hears this. Luckily, when I turn around, everyone's already down the hallway.

At Wreni's house, we set up the sweet karaoke machine she got for Christmas to her TV and connect her mP3 player.

We're scrolling through the options when I spot "Girls Just Want To Have Fun."

"That's it!" I shout.

"Good eyes!" Wreni presses the remote control button to highlight the title.

"It totally makes your toes start tapping on their own." Also, it's a song Mom loved when she was a kid and the smiley kind she would have sung back in her band days.

"Yeah it does!"

I love that Wreni is as excited about it as me.

We watch a bunch of videos on YouTube to get ideas for our dancing during the instrumental breaks.

It's actually not all that hard, it turns out, because the whole idea is just to show that we're having a blast. So we spin and clap in sync.

The thing about songs that aren't meant to be duets is that you have to alternate lead roles. But we get it down pretty awesome, actually, not to toot our own horns but seriously, it's not too bad.

I check the time in the corner of the computer screen and realize that it's been six hours since I left my house.

"Hey, Wreni, toss me my phone, will ya?" I ask over the music.

Wreni leans on one leg, knee bent and slides the

other leg beside it and claps. She spins and tosses the phone to me.

That move was totally stupid, wasn't it?" She asks after I hang up with Dad. He tells me that Mom's taking a nap.

"No, it was good."

"Riiight." Wreni smirks.

"Okay, it was kinda dumb," I admit.

"How about this?" Wreni busts into the worst dancing ever with arms flailing and legs kicking.

"C'mon, learn from the pro." I kick a leg up and we start the world's worst dance off.

While running in place, I move my arms like I'm swimming then move them closer together.

Wreni yells, "Oh my God, you look like a wounded deer!"

We fall to the floor at the same time, because you can't breathe or speak when you're in a hysterical frenzy.

I hold my side because my insides are twisting. That's what happens when laughing muscles don't get worked out often enough.

We rehearse the song and dance moves until we've got it totally memorized. Mrs. Hammer says it's "incredible" and I don't think she's just being nice.

She offers to drive me home. But she'll want to meet Mom and what if Mom's in a bad condition?

"Oh, that's okay," I say. "My mom is just getting

over the flu so it's better if you avoid our house!" I giggle for effect. I am getting good at this and that is not good.

When Dad calls to say he'll be there in ten minutes, Mrs. Hammer walks me to the front door and says, "Easter, you're welcome to come over anytime, okay?"

I whisper, "Thank you."

• • • TWENTY-THREE

There's a lot to do around the house. Just two days before Wreni comes over!

It's been three years since I had a friend visit. Stephanie was always over back then, especially in the summer. What was extra great about Stephanie is that we were kind of in our own world. We were cool with that. It wasn't that we didn't want to hang out with the other kids, it was just that that it was so much more fun with each other. She has three little brothers so I think she enjoyed less noise. And Yoplait. And Amigo. She would have liked Cindy, too, but I didn't have her back then. Her parents wouldn't allow pets. I'm lucky with that, I guess.

But then she moved. Far away.

If you think of Michigan as a giant mitten, she moved all the way to the top of your pinky. And we're at the base of the thumb.

When you don't have the Internet on your cell phone, it's pretty hard to keep in touch.

For a good three weeks, Stephanie and I lived for those daily calls but each week, month and year tugged us further apart and now birthday calls are all that's left.

She has a best friend up there named Carrie or Chrissie or something like that. I'm sure she's great but most of me hates her, though I've never met her. See, she has the only best friend I ever had (not counting Yoplait, of course).

Thinking about this stings more than the cleaning solution around my fingers as I scrub the bathroom counter.

I mop the floor, too, and I'm really on a roll, so soon, three hours are good and gone.

Yoplait sniffs my hand, drops her mouth and trots away with pee-u disgust.

By eight, Dad's still working so I wrap his plate of macaroni and cheese and sliced tomatoes with tin foil.

Diiiiing.

I lean over the counter and squint to see on the caller ID display that it's Aunt Deb who has the exact same hair and nose as Mom.

"It's Aunt Deb," I say but Mom doesn't hear on account of opening the sliding glass door and stepping onto the deck. She's bundled in her bathrobe and winter coat. She takes a sip of wine and I scoot around the counter to reach the phone. She doesn't stay out there long these days but Mom still makes a point of having a cigarette out there even when there's still snow. I guess she likes the fresh air.

"Hello?"

"Easter?"

"Yes."

"Hi, it's Aunt Deb," she says slowly like she's about to dump some bad news.

"Hiii."

"Are you doing all right, sweetie?"

"Uh yeah, why?"

"Oh your mom hasn't been returning my calls and I, well, I just got worried about you guys out there."

"Mmm hmm, everything's fine," I say in my most confident voice.

Out of the corner of my eye, I catch Yoplait two inches from the sliding glass door, which is open enough to fit her head through to the deck.

"Yo—Hang on, Aunt Deb!"

Clink. The phone hits the counter and I hear a faded "Easter?"

I lunge in two big steps and grab Yoplait with one hand on her back and the other under her belly. I scoot her backward and slide the door closed so fast, it rattles.

"No, Yoplait." I'm stern. "No, girl." I'm softer this time.

I knock on the glass and mouth, "Mooom, you left

the door open again."

Mom shouts, "It's not my fault that cat's so wild."

"It's winter, Yoplait, not summer. You won't like it out there!" I whisper toward the floor.

"Sorry about that, Aunt Deb," I say when I return to the phone. Please, please don't ask.

"Oh no problem, sweetie pie." It bugs me how she makes me feel like a little kid. "Is your mom there?"

I wince.

"Uh, yeah but she's out shoveling snow." I'm sorry to have to lie to you, it's just that you'll worry more if I tell the truth.

"Oh."

"Come here, Yoplait," I whisper.

"Easter, do you have my phone number in case you ever need to, you know, just chat or anything."

"Mmm hmm."

"Okay, good. Seriously, anytime. Even really late or really early. Anytime."

"Got it, thanks."

"Great, sweetie. So how's schoo—"

"Okay, Aunt Deb, well, I'll talk to you later and I'll tell Mom that you called."

"Alright, thanks, Easter."

"Bye!"

I press the off button before she gets a chance to say more.

The chair in my room is a major part of my nightly routine: I snuggle into it with a book, stuff my fuzzy blue blanket neatly in place under my legs and on cue, Yoplait appears in my lap where she sits, wrapping her tail around her body to make a complete circle. Only tonight I'm trying to read but can't. I keep imagining the forgotten open door and Yoplait chasing an animal out into the woods. Then never finding her way back. Since I have to go to school, I decide that there's only one solution to keep her safe.

Litter boxes are heavier than you'd think, especially when you have the basement steps plus the regular steps to deal with.

In the corner of my room, I lay two newspapers down and set the box atop. Yoplait does a sniff over to confirm it is in fact her box. Then, she takes advantage of its convenient new location and sits in there and does her business.

I pour her food and fill a bowl of water and set it all up under my bed but out of Amigo's reach so that she'll have everything she'll need—all safe and sound in my room when I'm not here.

In case she wants to sit at my window, I layer the sill with two towels so it's nice and comfy.

Later, after Mom's in bed, I'm sitting on my floor with jabbing worries. Again, those stupid what-ifs hanging around in my head.

What if Mom forgets about picking Wreni and me

up from school?

Sticky note reminders! Perfect. I make ten of them.

"Pick up Easter and Wreni at school." I put this one in the bathroom.

"Hi Mom! Today's Friday. See you at 2:45 at school. Super excited." This one's good for the coffeemaker.

I stick them everywhere Mom will go, even two on the door and two on the coffeemaker.

In the morning, I make sure my bedroom door is closed and Yoplait is sleeping safe inside, before I leave.

• • • TWENTY-FOUR

Worry blankets my brain again and when the dismissal bell rings, I shuffle out the door, forgetting to walk out with Wreni.

"Hey!" Wreni taps my shoulder.

"Hey!" It must be a lame hey because Wreni says, "What's wrong?"

"Nothing!" It's sharp so I soften it with, "Just zoned out."

We take a spot at the pickup curb and I scoot brown slush around with my boot.

Within a few minutes, all of the buses are gone and half of the kids crowded around are gone, too.

Please hurry up, Mom!

I don't want Wreni to worry so I ramble on about Mrs. Martin, Yoplait and anything else that pops into my head.

When there's a pause, Wreni spins around three hundred and sixty degrees on her patent leather shoes and says, all casual, "So what color car does your mom have?"

"Grey."

"Oh, okay." She makes a hand visor over her face and looks toward the road.

A fifth grader who's also waiting calls her mom and then Wreni says, "You want to call her?"

"Sure," I say upbeat.

So I dial Mom's cell and when the voicemail greeting comes on, I turn away from Wreni and say, "Mom, you must be on your way. We're waiting at the school." Click. I leave the same message on the house phone.

"She's probably on her way here now," Wreni says.

"Yeah, totally." I nod but I know better. I can tell by the topsy-turvy feeling inside me.

Mrs. Ritz asks me, "You both waiting for your mother?"

"Yes," we say at the same time.

"Then, you'll have to come in and I'll have to call your emergency contacts. It's too cold out here."

My face can't feel the cold; it's burning. Couldn't she have just said parents, rather than emergency contacts? It's not an emergency, yet.

"How 'bout calling your dad?" Mrs. Ritz asks.

"Sure."

We dial his cell and I leave a short message: "Dad,

Mom's not here to drive Wreni and me. We need to get picked up." He's probably in a meeting.

Click.

I'm so mad, I don't notice right away that Wreni's on the phone with her mom.

After a bit, Wreni's mom pulls up.

"Hey, girls!" She's so normal and mom-ish.

"Thanks so much for picking us up," I whisper.

It smells like apples and cinnamon inside her minivan and I look for it, but there's not a clump of dirt anywhere.

I give Mrs. Hammer directions but in my head, I'm going over everything about Mom and what's going on at home. Please, please don't humiliate me in front of Wreni and her mom.

Snow slushes around as we make our way down the street.

"I bet your mom was busy cleaning or something and lost track of time," Mrs. Hammer says because she is so nice.

"Yeah, probably." My voice quivers as we pull into the driveway.

"Ruff. Ruff. Ruff!" Amigo doesn't recognize the minivan and in the living room window, he's trying out his best tough dog act. The blinds sway and his nose is pressed against the glass, making round fog smudges that appear and disappear with each ruff.

"I'll walk you in," she says, "so your mom can meet me." But I know she wants to make sure everything's all right, too.

"Oh no, it's okay. She's probably taking a nap or something."

"Oh, I'll just come to the porch and you can go in and let me know all is fine. Okey dokey?"

"Sure." You really shouldn't argue much more with a grownup so I quiet myself.

So the three of us walk to the front porch and Amigo settles down a bit when he sees me. When I get to the door, it's unlocked but I open it only enough to peek inside. There's rattling in the kitchen. A lot of it. Like pots and pans being rummaged around.

Bamn. A cabinet door slams.

"Mom?" I put one foot forward and step into the foyer.

She jumps.

"Easter! Don't scare me like that!"

There are Tupperware containers and bowls and pots and pans and lots of cooking things scattered around.

I want to just close the door and run into my room. Even if Wreni and Mrs. Hammer think it's rude, at least they wouldn't see Mom like this.

"I can't find the casserole dish," she mumbles.

"Oh!" I ignore her. "Sorry, I just need you to meet Mrs. Hammer." I say it loud and extra slowly so she'll pick up on the fact that I'm not alone behind the door.

"Huh?" She just stares—confused, almost mad.

"Please," I mouth, open the door and take a deep

breath. "I said, Mrs. Hammer is here with Wreni." I point behind me.

This is fatal. I cannot bear to face them.

Amigo greets them and Wreni stoops and he gives her a slobbery kiss.

Mrs. Hammer waves her friendliest to Mom, who's totally confused. Mom steps forward into the hallway, nearly tripping on the cookware and looks at me like I've done something wrong.

"Reeemember, you were supposed to pick Wreni and me up after school to go to the thrift store?" I say this politely but bug out my eyes.

"What? You never told me that was today!" Mom shakes her head.

"Yes, I did," I say softly because I don't want her to argue.

"Oh well, another time for sure." Mrs. Hammer is smiling, polite and awkward, I can tell, though I can't bear to turn around.

Mom doesn't say a word more so we all stand there in horrible silence.

Then Mrs. Hammer says, "Well, Easter, it was very nice to see you again" and puts her hand on my shoulder. I know it'd be rude to not turn so I do, but just a few inches. Tears gloss my eyes and I'm fighting a wail. Wreni and Mrs. Hammer both give pity/worry looks but I force a smile.

"Thanks so much, Mrs. Hammer, for driving me home."

Then I turn to Wreni and say, "See ya at school."

"Yep," she says, "I'll see you in the morning!" and her eyes dart back to Mom and then into the kitchen to the cooking stuff and then to an open bottle of wine atop the counter.

I wish I could zap myself to my room right at this very second but I say "okay," nudge Amigo away from the door and close it before they've even turned toward the street.

"Easter!"

I sprint up the stairs to my room without a word to Mom, though she hollers my name twenty times in a row.

• • • TWENTY-FIVE

"Yoplait?!"

My bedroom door is open halfway. The hall's never seemed so long as I take three long sprints in fast motion.

"Yoplait?!" I kneel at my bed, lift my bedskirt and scan between board games and photo albums. "Yoplait!"

My whole body shakes like I'm freezing and melting at the same time.

"Roooooof." Amigo stands in the doorway, shifting his weight from paw to paw and moving his eyes around the room. He knows—and he's sick with worry, too.

"Amigo, where is she? Where's Yoplait?"

His ears fold back and he locks eye contact like, "I'm sorry, I don't know, I'm sorry."

In my closet, I toss out five pairs of boots in case she's snuggled up between them. I shine a flashlight behind my bed.

"Yooooplait!" I shout from the hallway.

Think think think.

In Mom and Dad's room, I flip on the ceiling light and repeat the same steps.

Even in the hallway bathroom closet, behind the shower curtain, everywhere.

Downstairs, Mom's curled up on the couch—with all of the pots and pans still spread out.

In the basement, I'm louder. "Please, Yoplait, where are you?!"

"Mom!" I shout on the top of my lungs as I sprint up the steps. "My cat is…" I choke. "My cat is goooone."

"Rooool!" Amigo breaks the silence. Tears fall fast as I reach for the kitchen phone.

I dial as fast as I can.

"Easter?" Dad answers on ring three. "Hang on. I'll call you back." And another phone closes. "Yes, Easter?"

"Dad!" I try to stay calm but it's impossible.

"Hi. Why aren't you at school?"

"School's out for the day," I say, "It's almost four."

I picture him checking his watch.

"Oh, you're right. Time flies here. What's the matter?"

"Wreni Hammer's mom had to drive me home

because Mom never showed up," I say before I have a chance to change my mind. "I already left you a message!"

He sighs and says, "Is that right?!"

"Yes! But the worst part is," I choke, "Yoplait's gone!" Be brave. It's no use. I flip the phone up away from my mouth and sob.

"Easter, I'm leaving now."

"Dad," shakes from my lips, "please help me find her. Please!"

"Yes, I'm leaving now."

"C'mon, Amigo," I stand and tap him on the shoulder to say follow me.

I grab his leash hanging on the doorknob and clip it to his collar when we're on the porch.

"Let's find her!" I say all confident like a detective.

From the driveway, we run—fast.

"Yoplait!" I shout every five feet.

Near the woods and in front of Drama Chihuahua's house, I shout extra loud.

Amigo trots in step with me, even throwing in a ruff to help.

When I'm a grownup, I tell myself, I will never live on a Street O' Old People like this ever. There's no one to ask for help in finding a cat who thinks she's a dog.

At the end of the street, near the lake, Amigo slows to a walk.

Vvvroooom. We both jump back from the road to

avoid a too-close-to-the-side-of-the-road motorcycle.

My heart beats so fast, it covers up my lungs and I can hardly breathe.

Amigo sits and his tongue drips. He stares up at me like now what?

Waves of nausea hit my stomach faster than the two cars that speed by.

"Yoplait's out there!" I explain to Amigo.

I kick three rocks into the street.

"C'mon, Amigo, c'mon!"

We rush home, get my bike and spend the next twenty minutes riding up and down the streets, calling for Yoplait.

In the kitchen, I wait. I'd planned for macaroni and cheese for dinner with Wreni but I'm not about to cook it so I put the box into the pantry.

I watch the clock tick. Dad finally arrives.

"Sue?" Dad calls the second he comes through the door. He yells it three more times before Mom rises from the couch like a zombie.

Just like that, Dad knows that things are worse than I've let him see.

"What are you doing home?" She looks at me and then back at Dad.

"What happened here today?" His face is tight.

I sit on the floor between the dining room and the living room and wrap my arms around Amigo.

"What?" She seriously looks like she doesn't know.

My eyes close tight.

"Sue, you're drunk! In the middle of the day!"

Mom stomps upstairs.

Dad paces around the living room and for a solid five minutes, shouts one-word sentences to himself like "unacceptable" and "unfit mother."

I rest my head on my hands. After a bit, I hear Dad upstairs, opening and closing cabinets, drawers and closet doors. He finds full bottles somewhere and pours them down the sink in the bathroom. I can tell by the cling clanging.

He passes me in the kitchen on his way to the garage.

"Unacceptable!" He shouts again to no one and drops the bag of bottles to the bottom of the garbage can so roughly, I worry that the bottles will shatter.

Amigo puts two paws on my lap and licks my arm.

"Dad," I whisper, fighting back tears, "please help me find Yoplait. Please."

"Yes, Easter, later, we'll make some phone calls."

Then I get mad at myself. I never should have called Dad home.

"Dad!" I scream so loud as I stand, I shake. "Pleeeeasse." Tears soak my hands.

Dad stops in the laundry room doorway and says with softness, "Easter, honey, calm down. It's going to be okay."

But he doesn't even offer to drive around and look for her.

"No, Dad!" I shout and the stool beneath me crashes to the tile. "This is important to me! Please!"

I sob the soaking kind, holding my face in my hands and Dad's saying something but I'm crying too hard to hear.

I run to my room and slam the door. Mom hollers something from down the hall.

I'm so alone.

Guardian angel, hi, yoo hoo. Need you. I don't have anyone to ask for help.

Without waiting to calm myself, I kneel on the floor and dial Wreni's cell but there's no answer so I call her house phone.

"Hello?"

"Mrs. H-h-hammer?"

"Yes! Easter?"

"Yes, hi, um, I'm sorry to bother you," I try my hardest to sound normal but it's pretty impossible when you're in the midst of hysterical crying, "But my cat, Yoplait, is missing. I, we, can't find her."

"Oooh no, honey! Do you want us to come help you look?"

"No, it's okay, I just thought I'd tell you so you could keep your eyes open,"

"Hang on, sweetheart," Mrs. Hammer says.

"Easter!" Wreni says after a minute or so. "We're going looking around town for her. I'll call you, okay?"

"Really?!" I have never felt more grateful.

"Yeah, she can't be far."

"Okay, thank you, thank you," I whisper.

"It's going to be alright, honey," Mrs. Hammer says from another phone.

"Thank you." Click.

I say one hundred prayers in a row. My heart finally slows to a semi-normal beat.

I stay in my room the rest of the night, pretending to be asleep.

At some point, I hear Mom's car start up and zoom down the road.

• • • TWENTY-SIX

The next morning, I wake to Dad knocking at my door.

"Uh huh?" croaks from my dry throat.

Dad steps in, sending a beam of hallway light into the room and Amigo, next to me in Yoplait's spot, rolls over to face the wall.

"Hi, hun," he says, cupping the phone receiver and holding it out to me, "For you. Wreni."

Out the window goes any shred of hope that it was all a nightmare.

"News about Yoplait?!" I whisper and sit up fast.

He shakes his head no.

I put my hands on my neck to motion that my throat hurts.

"Are you sure?" He whispers.

I nod.

"Wreni? I'm sorry but Easter's still sleeping. She'll call you back later…uh huh, yes, sure thing. Goodbye." Click.

"She's worried, Easter."

I slump back.

"I'll make breakfast," Dad says and pats his leg to signal Amigo to follow.

"Where's Mom?" I ask when he turns.

"She came home early this morning," he says sad and angry all mixed together.

I go downstairs, tell Dad I'm going to go to Wreni's after all, and he smiles, like 'good.' Wreni answers her cell phone with, "Hi Easter! We're going to drive around looking for Yoplait again this morning!"

"Hey." I move the receiver away from my face so she can't hear that I'm fighting a major cry. "Oh thanks so much!"

"I was thinking we could make lost cat signs and put them around. My mom says she'll pick you up and we can do that and then go shopping for our Talent Show outfits."

"That would be great. I would love that."

"Sweet! How's like an hour from now? We'll pick you up. Oh, and bring a photo of Yoplait with you."

"Okay."

Mrs. Hammer doesn't mention or ask about the whole Mom thing. Phew. She just talks about all of the places that Yoplait could be.

At her house, we scan the photo and print fifty copies. With fat markers, Mrs. Hammer, Wreni and I sit at their kitchen table and decorate as many posterboards as we can. On Main Street, we give them to the business owners to post. We staple them to poles.

• • • TWENTY-SEVEN

Dad picks me up from Wreni's and he's pretty quiet the whole way home, giving me time to think about Mom for the first time since the incident. Waves of fuming anger settle into nausea. This repeats again and again all the way until we're home and when I see her, I feel plain old anger send away the sickness.

When we pass in the kitchen, she says "hi" but today, I'm really not up for conversation so I go right to my room.

On the Status page of Operation Cool, I write, "Operation Cool is no longer the majorly important thing in my life" and underline it.

I go to sleep without dinner and in the middle of the night, I'm awakened from half sleep by Mom firing swear words at Dad. I pull my comforter over my head and wrap my arms around my pillow and squeeze it.

"Please, please, make things get better," I whisper in the dark.

In the morning, I'm making a PB & J sandwich for my lunch when Mom enters and goes directly to the coffeemaker.

I don't bother with a "morning."

Mom studies my outfit: faded jeans and sparkly pink sweater. I see her in the corner of my eye. "You look cute."

"Thanks," I mumble and stuff the sandwich into a plastic bag.

"You want me to take you to the thrift store after school today?"

"I already went with Wreni yesterday." I pretend to concentrate on perfectly arranging the contents of my lunch bag.

"We could go together."

"I have rehearsal for the Talent Show," I snap. "I've only had the sheet with that info hanging on the fridge for weeks now." I roll my eyes for effect and don't even regret it.

"Oh." She fiddles with the strings of her sweatshirt hood and bites her bottom lip. For a second or two, I feel sorry for her like she's a bear who's just woken up from winter hibernation and is totally out of the loop on everything.

I once saw an interview with a Broadway actress.

She said she doesn't really get nervous performing in front of a packed theater but those rehearsals with just a few key people are terrifying.

I'm thinking about this at rehearsal when Mrs. Martin says, "Okay, Easter and Wreni, you're up next." Get-me-out-of-this schemes are whirring around in my head including telling Mrs. Martin that I am about to ralph up my lunch or that I took cold medicine so I'm not in the right state of mind to do this now.

But I can't disappoint Wreni. She's a little nervous, too. I can tell because she's shifting around in her chair. What does she have to be nervous about? She's already perfect.

We're in the Talent Show together. Holy macaroni.

By the time we're on stage, four feet apart and microphones in hand, my knees are knocking together.

"No biggie, girl," Wreni whispers to me just as Mrs. Martin presses play on the music system.

Surprisingly, the words flow out of my mouth and by my second turn to sing, my legs and arms loosen enough to move as planned and the audience of twenty or so follows.

During the instrumental break of the song, Wreni and I shimmy, slide and clap to the beat and criss cross on the edge of the stage. The crowd roars, well, as much as a crowd of that size can.

• • • TWENTY-EIGHT

A half an hour before we're supposed to leave for the Talent Show, Mom announces that she's feeling too sick to go, just yet.

Dad's mad. There's yelling.

Since I have to be there early, I tell Dad I'll ask Mrs. Hammer to swing by and pick me up on their way to the school.

He nods and says they'll see me there.

My heart's beating double time and the butterflies who've been hanging around inside a lot lately have officially multiplied into a whole village.

A sixth grader and his older brother are shuffling around and kicking in karate attire on a thick mat across the stage.

Mrs. Martin stands besides Wreni and me on the

side, behind the red velvet curtain.

All I can do is think about what's happening at home.

"Look out! Karaaahtaaay time!" Wreni puts her arms up like she's going to hi-yaaah something right in half.

I force a smile but it's unconvincing.

"C'mon, Easter. Loosen it up." She flails her arms around like she did in our goofball dance off.

Best friends are handy for cheering you up or at least shooing away the worry thoughts, just like that.

I don't actually hear the audience clapping at the close of the karate brothers.

We step out onto the stage after the karate brothers fold up their mat and slide it behind the curtain.

I've read that it's best to not make eye contact with the audience but I really can't miss Grandma Dottie with her ruby red lipstick in the front row between waving Aunt Deb and two empty seats.

Where's Mom? Where's Dad?

Breathe, I remind myself.

The music starts and Wreni and I clap and tap our heels against the stage.

I notice there's a dark triangle between the golden spotlights, just big enough to see the set of double doors in the back of the gym. One opens slowly. There may be a creaking sound; I can't hear. Dad steps through and turns around to make the door close without sound.

No Mom! Where is she?

My brain processes a thousand "what ifs," while singing and shuffling from foot to foot, which if you tried it, you'd know it's a hard thing to do.

That's when the words and dance moves etched into my brain fly far, far away. I'm frozen on stage. Jaw locks. Legs are statue solid. The eyes of the audience dart from Wreni and stick to me. I'm paused this way until Wreni finishes the song, including all of my parts. When everyone claps and Wreni curtsies and tries to get my attention for the billionth time, I run off the stage, across the gym and out the doors to the hallway.

I made a complete fool of myself!

Need air.

I sprint through the front doors onto the blacktop. The air is stingy cold so I rub my arms.

Guardian angel, yoo hoo, over here! Need you for a minute, again. I close my eyes and take a deep breath.

Disappear into the darkness, that's what I'd like to do right about now. The image of Wreni's disappointed face won't get out of my mind. I let her down.

"Easter."

I ignore because the last thing I want to do is talk to anyone.

"Easter." It's Connor.

"Please, please leave me alone right now." I wipe away tears and hold my arms.

"I was just going to tell you it was really awesome,

your performance in there."

"Are you kidding me?!" I snap in I-can't-stand-you tone. "I froze!"

"But you did great until that moment. Seriously!"

I bite my lip.

"I think people would have loved to see your photos, too."

"Connor, just stop." I put my hand up like a crossing guard, then fold my arms tighter and walk five feet away so he knows I'm done talking. "No one cares about my stupid photos."

He sucks in a deep breath.

"Easter, do you know what the definition of insanity is?"

I sigh, like 'What the heck does that have to do with anything.'

"Einstein said it's doing the same thing over and over again and expecting a different result."

I snap my head up to stare at the stars, without looking at him, like please just stop talking.

"If things are out of control in your life, you have to step up and get help. There are some things you just can't fix on your own, ya know."

I sniffle a few times before a real cry comes and when I try to hold it back, it shakes my whole body. My arms are cold without a jacket so I rub my hands over them fast.

The sound of quick footsteps grows.

"Easter!" Dad calls.

I don't respond.

"Thanks, Connor," Dad whispers. He must have nodded, like 'I've got it from here,' because Connor's shoes hit the pavement in the direction of the school.

"I'm sorry I was late, Easter," Dad whispers behind me and puts his hand on my shoulder.

I step to the right fast so his hand falls off.

"Easter, I was late because I had to meet one of my employees on Main—"

"What?!" I spin around and unfold my arms to make a wide are-you-kidding-me gesture. "Everything is spinning out of control and you're doing work stuff?!"

"Easter," Dad says ultra-soft.

"No, Dad! My only true friend. The only one I can totally count on. She's gone! I can't believe it. She was the only—" I can hardly breathe and each word comes out more muffled and weirder than the first. "And where's Mom?!"

Grandma Dottie and Aunt Deb are walking fast toward us. I know it's rude but I don't even want to say hello.

"Easter!" Dad shouts this time. "I was late because I was picking up Yoplait. One of the packaging guys found her giving a puppy a hard time outside of Scoops this afternoon."

"What?" I stop crying enough to hear.

"Yoplait's at home waiting patiently for your return." He smiles that ginormous ear-to-ear grin.

I leap, jump into Dad's arms and wrap my arms around his neck. He hugs me like he's a giant bear.

"Thank you. Thank you. Thank you," I whisper.

Something about this bear hug and looking at smiling Grandma Dottie and Aunt Deb makes me crumble inside. I tighten my eyes together and tears sneak out and after a few seconds, it turns into a major sob like a toddler does when she loses her balloon to the wind.

Dad holds me tighter.

"Easter, dear, is something else wrong?" Grandma Dottie whispers and rubs my arm.

Connor's words echo in my head: You have to step up and ask for help.

I let go of Dad's neck and he lowers me back to the ground.

Stop crying. Be brave.

"Mom's not doing well at all," I say to the pavement between catch-my-breath sniffles. "I can't keep hoping that she's going to get better. She's getting worse. Nothing I do changes it. I can't fix her!"

Aunt Deb steps forward and puts her arm across my shoulders and pulls me close. That's when all of it comes pouring out, in whisper tone.

"She's drinking. A lot." I swallow and run my hands under my eyes and wipe away the tears on my shirt. "And sleeping all day. And never talking to me. And I make macaroni and cheese a lot because she doesn't cook anything. And I empty the bottles and hide them in the garbage so Dad doesn't see. She's not the same person. I thought it would pass. I thought I could make her get better. I tried so hard. I can't do it." I cry hard like a newborn. It's not easy to breathe.

Aunt Deb sniffles and holds me very tight.

"I miss her. I miss my mom."

"I know, hun," she whispers.

"Easter," Dad says in that familiar tone like sad and mad mixed together. "Why didn't you tell me how bad things are?"

I look up for the first time in a long while. "Because I thought you'd divorce her!" Tears roll down my cheeks again. Grandma steps forward and pulls me in for a soft and cushiony hug.

"Do you want me to go back in and get your jacket for you, honey?" Dad asks.

"No, I just want to see Yoplait."

Grandma Dottie opens the door to Aunt Deb's shiny red compact car and slides in next to me in the backseat.

"Don't you worry your pretty little head anymore," Grandma Dottie says. "I'm so glad you've told us what's going on." She holds my ice-cold hands the whole way home.

It feels like a hundred million gallizion pounds were lifted from my shoulders.

"I promise you that we'll do whatever we can to help your mother," she says with confidence.

• • • TWENTY-NINE

Aunt Deb pulls in behind Dad's truck as Dad's walking through the front door at home.

In the foyer, Yoplait rushes to the doorway and Dad scoops her up and stands on the porch. He pets her head and under his arm, her giant tail whips back and forth.

Before the car's parked, I open the door and sprint across the lawn.

Yoplait leaps from Dad's arms into mine before I'm even up the stairs.

"Yoplait, hi, hi, hi!" I squeeze her tight when she rubs her face against my neck and her whiskers tickle. "I was so worried. I couldn't stop worrying about you."

She scoots up and rests her paws on my shoulder, purring so loudly, it vibrates her whole body.

Amigo runs from the front door and fast off of the porch to join the reunion.

"Rooooo!"

"I know, Amigo!" I pat his head with one hand. "She's back. Can you believe it? She's back!"

Inside, I don't even wonder where Mom is.

After Amigo and Yoplait gobble up dinner, I feel more tired than a kindergartener fighting heavy eyelids on New Year's Eve.

When Grandma tucks me in, I start to get comfy but say, "Oh, just a minute, I have to check on Mom."

"No, honey, that's okay. Your mama's fine and sleeping soundly, honey."

"Okay." My eyelids are too heavy to keep open anyway.

Amigo beats my alarm clock in waking me by over an hour. The smell of eggs and toast hits my nose and pulls me down to the kitchen where I find Amigo begging for bacon, despite Grandma completely ignoring him. He pulls out all the tricks. There's dancing, rolling over and play-dead begging. That means he's not going to give up until you cave in.

"Good morning, Easter dear!" Grandma says with I'm-so-happy-to-see-you enthusiasm.

"Morning, Gram."

"How are you feeling this morning?"

"Okay."

After my tummy is completely full, Grandma says,

"You don't have to go to school today, Easter. After the crazy night you had, I re—"

"No!" I shout so loud it startles Grandma. "Really," I continue softer, "I have to go."

"Oh, honey, I really think you ought to rest up."

"I have to work on Operation Cool," I say without thinking.

"Operation what, dear?" Grandma asks while rinsing a skillet in the sink.

I tell her everything that's happened recently, including about how Tommy Hansen actually only liked Wreni.

Grandma listens carefully and scrunches up her face at the Horse Girl parts.

Wreni. I let her down. Telling that part of the story stabs me in the heart.

"I have to go today so that I can explain to her. I didn't mean to let her down."

"She'll understand," Grandma Dottie says nodding. "Listen here, my darling, you are a smart, funny, caring, hilarious, amazing, unique girl who is LOVED by her parents more than anything in the world. And the problem your mother faces has nothing to do with you."

She gets really close to my face. "It's not your fault," she says and holds my wrists "It's not fair that you've gone through this. Thank you for telling us, sweetheart. You should have called me and told me right away. You were very brave and loving to try to fix the situation on your own. Now, we'll do whatever we can to help your mom."

I nod and slide off the stool.

Mom's still in bed when I crack open her door.

I don't whisper. I say aloud, "Hi, Mom."

She rolls over and pulls the comforter up closer to her face.

I can tell Wreni's surprised to see me get out of Dad's truck because she's waiting where the kids get off the bus.

"Hey!" She shouts, though we're too far apart to hear each other. She grips her purse to stop it from swaying as she runs across the parking lot to meet me.

I wave. Deep breath.

"Easter, I heard about Yoplait!" She says after a long hug. "I was so excited to hear that she's home, I almost cried!"

"I know! I'm so happy!"

"But are you okay?" she leans in and whispers close to my face.

"I'm fine, but I'm so, so sorry that I ruined everything at the Talent Show."

"Stop," she says. "I don't care about that. I want to know if you're okay, if your family is okay." She's worried. Her face is frown-y and tense in a way I've never seen before.

If I tell her about everything, she'll be worried for me. If I tell her about everything, she might feel sorry for me. If I tell her about everything, she might not want to be friends with me.

But she is my best friend.

I do not want to lie to my best friend.

So right there on the blacktop, I tell her about Mom, Dad, how things used to be, how they've been and how I hope they're going to be.

When I'm done, she simply smiles, hugs me and says, "You're not alone. I am always here for you and you for me. That is what makes me your best friend and you my best. Always share the truth."

I promise that I will.

This is shocking but no one mentions anything about my Talent Show escape.

It's because a girl tripped walking down the stage stairs and knocked down one of the teachers. That was the talk of the day.

• • • THIRTY

I hear Grandma Dottie's rusty Buick make its way from the road to the school parking lot.

It always sounds like the muffler's about to fall off, but Grandma says it just likes to make an entrance wherever it goes.

When I swing my backpack onto the floor of the passenger side, Grandma says, "Hi, Easter!" so loud, a dozen kids look up.

"Hi, Grandma," I say in a normal inside voice. I sit, shut the creaky door, pull my seatbelt and click it into place.

"Honey, we're going to make a stop before we go home."

"Okay." A lump thing forms in my belly for some reason.

Tick tock. Tick tock. Tick tock. The turn signal

sings until Grandma spins the wheel.

"There's a wonderful man I spoke to on the phone this morning," Grandma Dottie says.

She pauses like she's thinking hard.

"This man has spent the last twenty years helping families," she says, clears her throat and continues with upbeatness. "He helps those who are battling the same problem your mother has."

I lean my head against the window and grip the seatbelt.

"He is going to help us talk to your mother and see if we can get her to accept help. I know it's hard to understand what's going on with your mother, but what she's facing is actually quite common. Depression and alcoholism." She sighs. "There are so many people with these same problems."

I nod.

"The only way your mother can recover is if she agrees to get help. No one can make her do anything. That's the hardest part, honey."

At the church meeting room building, Dad opens the door before we reach it.

"Easter," he says in an extra sweet way like he did when I was super young. "Easter, honey."

He pulls me in for a hug. His shirt smells like Maggie Mae, but I don't mind a bit. I close my eyes and wrap my arms tight around him, just like I do with Yoplait and Amigo. But unlike pet hugs, Dad folds his arms around me and squeezes back. I peek around him, open my eyes and look inside to the hallway.

Standing there is a tall, thin man about forty something, with a friendly smile.

"So what are we doing?" I push free from Dad and step into the hallway near a meeting room.

"Hi, Easter!"

Aunt Deb walks across and I meet her halfway for a hug, like it's been a long time since I saw her last.

She's looking worried and even a little tear-y eyed but forcing a smile for me.

Grandma says, "We are all here to help your mother. Like you, we love her and want her to get better."

"This is Mr. Shelton, and he's an expert in helping people with problems like this," Dad says, pointing to the tall man.

"Hi, ya!" He has a 'hey-I-totally-understand-how-uncool-life-has-been-lately' expression. "I'm an intervention specialist, which means that I help loved ones show people with addictions and other destructive behavior how much they are affected by it. And help them get better." He smiles a big 'save-the-day' kind of smile and holds his hand out.

I shake it as confidently as I can.

"Thank you for helping us." I nod my head and wish with all my heart that this works.

Grandma grabs my hand and leads me to sit in a chair beside her at the table.

"Easter, this is going to be a lot to absorb, but

you're going to learn all about what's been going on with your mom," Mr. Shelton says as he pulls out a chair and sits. "She is in denial about her drinking problem. That means she doesn't want to admit that her body's dependent on alcohol to feel normal."

Aunt Deb clears her throat. "You just tell her, calmly, how you feel, honey, okay?" She smiles and pats my leg.

Guilt swirls around inside me about fibbing about Mom to her.

"Yes," Mr. Shelton says and taps his chest. "You just speak from the heart."

I nod and hold onto the bottom of my shirt.

"We're going to practice what we're going to say so that we're not at a loss for words when we're with Sue tonight," says Mr. Shelton.

Dad leans forward and the legs of his chair scrape against the tile.

"I'll go first," he says, sort of quiet and shy. "I'm going to tell her that I love her and that I'm sorry, I'm so sorry for not addressing her problems before now. I've failed as a husband and father in that way." He shakes his head and stares at the table.

"No, Dad," I shout. "It's my fault. I hid it from you!"

"Easter," Mr. Shelton interrupts. "Your intentions were wonderful. You were trying to be a loving daughter to your mother."

"I should have told you, Dad. I shouldn't have hid

the bottles." Tears fall before I can try to stop them.

Dad sighs and shakes his head. "Easter, honey, listen to me. You've done nothing wrong. I should have paid closer attention. You shouldn't have been put in the position of having to hide anything from me."

Mr. Shelton stands, grabs a box of tissue from a nearby table and sets it in front of me.

"Alcoholism is a disease," he says. "That's hard to believe when you first learn about it. Your mother was feeling broken inside and chose drinking to help her escape those sad feelings. Then her body got addicted to the alcohol and couldn't function right without it. By that point, the problem was too difficult to fix it on her own."

Grandma Dottie pulls out two tissues from the box and hands one to me.

We each speak about our worries and how much we miss Mom. The old version of her.

"But where is Mom?" I ask when Dad pulls into the driveway of our house.

"She's with Uncle Jeff. Went for a quick coffee."

Inside we sit around the living room in the seats we planned. Everyone has shifty eyes, even Amigo, who is unusually quiet, despite having so many visitors with foreign scents and worried faces.

The lump thing does a summersault in my tummy.

"When Sue arrives, she might be angry," Mr.

Shelton says as he scans the room. "She might be sad. She might try to leave. She definitely won't be happy. We just want her to know that we're here to help her overcome her problems, if she'll let us."

Bam. A car door shuts in the driveway.

Uncle Jeff is first to come in. He stands there a few seconds before Mom follows him in.

I wish it were just a birthday party, but there's no "surprise!" to shout, nor clapping and rushing to greet her.

Mom looks surprised, she really does, though she probably had half an idea, with all the cars in the driveway.

She even sort of smiles, but it fades quickly when she sees Mr. Shelton.

I feel sorry for her, like she's being ganged up on.

Dad gestures to the big cushiony chair for Mom to sit.

Mom doesn't sit, just backs up toward the front door and shakes her head in an irritated way, like we've all turned out to be traitors worse than foreign spies.

"Hello Sue, I'm Mr. Shelton." He puts out his hand to shake, but Mom refuses.

"Unbelievable," she mumbles.

"I'm here to help your family tell you how much they love you and why they are very worried about you."

She opens the front door and has one foot on the porch when I shout, "Wait!"

"Mom," I say more softly. "Please stay for this." She pulls her foot back in, slams the door, and waits a few seconds with her back to us before turning to face everyone again.

"This is ridiculous," she says, gritting her teeth, not to me, but directly to Dad, who is staring at the carpet. She sits on the edge of the chair.

I don't realize that I'm shaking until Grandma Dottie links her arms with mine and holds my hand.

Aunt Deb and Uncle Jeff describe their worries about Mom. They end with the same conclusion— they miss the old Sue. The same one I love and miss, too.

Grandma Dottie's next and she sniffles through it, telling us all how much she wants to make Mom feel better.

"Sue, I can only imagine how much pain you must feel inside," she says. "It has broken my heart to see you feeling this way. You've always been such a wonderful mother. And now..." Grandma pauses and looks at me. "This is really impacting your family."

All the while, Mom keeps her head down, shaking her head and adding 'oh-please-you're-all-exaggerating' comments, even smirking at times, as if it were a comedy show.

Dad goes next.

"Sue, I have to say I know I should have done something sooner." He swallows. Mom finally looks up. "I know you've been battling this on your own for a year or so. I didn't take the time to see what was happening. I should have listened better. I should have asked more questions. I'm so sorry."

Then he wipes away tears! My dad is crying! I've never, ever seen that in my life. He looks more like a dad and less like a corporate director of quality control than ever!

"Things are not going to turn around on their own, Sue. You need more help than that. I think we both know that. I'm sorry I didn't realize this sooner, honey."

I wish a light bulb would turn on inside Mom's head and she would understand it all suddenly and jump up and kiss Dad. But she says nothing.

Then it is my turn. I take a really deep breath.

"Mom." I remind myself to look directly at her, but she's still staring at the carpet, so I say gently, "Mom, please." Her head rises slowly, and for the first time in a long, long while, she listens.

"I never realized what a fantastic mom I had." I wipe away tears before they fall. Be brave. "Until that mom disappeared and left me with a barely alive mom. I feel, I feel like I've lost the real you forever. Only it's worse, because I worry ALL THE TIME about you—this version of you—whoever you are these days."

I press my face into Grandma Dottie's sweater, though it's itchy and perfume-y, and I cry the wailing kind that shakes your whole body. I look up and right then, it's like Mom's bones fall apart. She collapses back into the chair and makes a tent over her face with her hands. And she cries, too. Hard.

Everyone in the room sniffles, too, and Mr. Shelton seems relieved to see Mom finally responding.

I've never witnessed so many people crying at once. I stand up and sit right next to Mom on her chair, just like I did as a kid, and hold on to her. I feel like a grownup but still a kid at the same time and I don't want to let go.

"Sue," Mr. Shelton interrupts gently. "Let us help you." There's no snarky response or eye rolling this time. She just wipes her eyes with Grandma Dottie's tissue.

That's when Dad heads up stairs. I listen to the creaky steps all the way to their room. He appears a few minutes later with a stuffed duffle bag.

"Let's go, Sue."

"Now?!" Mom shouts so abruptly Grandma Dottie and I both jump.

"Yes, now," Dad says, gently, though his face is stern and his lips are tight.

"No, I need time to get things together and I thi—"

"Already packed and set to go," Dad says in an upbeat way as he raises the duffle bag high in the air.

I stand and Mom slumps back in the chair, resting her arms on the sides and shooting Dad an eyes-locked, 'absolutely-not' look.

"Sue," Grandma says. "I really think it's best for you to—"

"Please stay out of it." Mom's eyes never move from Dad.

"It's the best of the best addiction recovery centers in the state, honey, you know that," Dad says. "Just three weeks."

And then, right then, I have a rush of bravery.

"Mom, please, for me. Please!" I say it over and over and over again, making it clear I won't stop until she agrees to go.

And then she does, after the world's longest hug with me.

Mr. Shelton and Dad drive away with her and I wave on the front porch.

Grandma Dottie, Uncle Jeff and Aunt Deb tell me I did a great job and that it's because of me that Mom's going to get better.

Yoplait meets me in the hallway and meows a "good job," too.

• • • THIRTY-ONE

I wake the next day to Grandma Dottie mo\
around pots and pans in the kitchen cabinets.

She makes the most amazing French toast with
extra cinnamon-y goodness. It's just about the most
awesome breakfast ever. We cave and give Amigo a
couple of pieces, which he inhales, Scooby Doo style.
You just can't say no to a dancing dog.

Grandma Dottie's car pulls up to school just as the
buses are unloading, and when I open the car door,
Connor is stepping off of the bus. It's one of those
freaky situations where we look at each other at the
exact same moment. He waves and I nearly slam my
skirt in the door as I wave back.

"Bye, Grandma!" I shout, though the door's already
shut.

I'm at least two yards away when I hear the window

g behind me. Grandma must be rolling it

ut Connor is on his way over, so I walk toward

hat'd you say, sweetheart?"

pin around. Grandma Dottie's draped over the

enger seat with her ginormous sunglasses sliding

n her nose. "Oh, just 'bye' Grandma."

"Whaaat?"

"I was just saying goodbye," I say louder.

"Oh, okay, honey. Have a wonderful day! Oh, who's your cute friend?" She winks and points behind me.

I shut my eyes fast, then turn around slowly to see Connor waving.

"Hi, Easter's grandma!" he says, showing off his dimples, because he's the kind of guy to be actually happy to meet somebody's grandma.

"Hello, dear! Who are you?" Without giving him a millisecond to respond, she says, "Oh, I know, I bet you're Connor!"

My face burns at a minimum of nine thousand degrees.

"Yes, I'm Connor," he says and put his hands in his pockets, because that's what you do when you get put on the spot.

"That's nice. Alrighty, you two have a great day!"

She presses too hard on the gas pedal and her car takes off superfast. The tires make a screechy sound.

Everyone in front of the school stares, which

makes Connor and me crack up.

"She's awesome," he says.

"Yeah, I know. She's the best."

"Cool for a grandma."

"Totally," I say.

We start toward the front door and a good ten seconds pass while I search for something else to say.

"Hey," we both say turning to each other at the same time.

"Yeah?" I say quickly. "Oh, you first."

"No, you go ahead."

"Um, well, I forgot now what I was going to say."

"Oh, I was just going to say I'm sorry for getting on your case about showing people your photos. I just think they're really good."

"No, no, I'm the one who should apologize. I shouldn't have snapped at you. You were only being nice."

"Nah, don't sweat that. I butted in. But I'd like to have some of them. You know, use them as a screensaver on my laptop and stuff. Will you give me some of them?"

"Sure, I can email a bunch to you today during Advisory."

"Awesome!"

"Hey!" Wreni stuffs her cell into her pocket and runs to meet me. It feels good to have someone wait for you before school.

"Whoa, awesome shirt, girl!"

I pull the bottom and stare down at the cartoon cat on my shirt. "Thanks! Yeah, it's awesome, isn't it?"

"Yeah!"

I hear Horse Girl's voice. My heart slides to my belly.

"Niiice shirt! I wondered what happened to the pajama shirt I wore in kindergarten."

Some kids laugh and face her, creating a perfect pathway for her to approach.

I ignore her and hope that if I just keep talking to Wreni, Horse Girl will quiet on her own.

But Wreni says, "Shut your mouth, Erica!" and tugs on my sleeve to walk in the other direction, but I don't move.

I shake my head and hold my jaw tight.

The whole crowd quiets and their eyes dart from Horse Girl to Wreni to me and back.

I search my brain for anything. It doesn't have to be funny. Just something.

"Man, you gotta get out of your house," Horse Girl says, like it's the most hilarious joke of her life and stares right into my eyes. "Or you're totally gonna turn into a cat lady who wears cat shirts all of the time."

A couple of kids crack up behind her.

"Whatever, Erica," I say as confidently as I can. "At least I wear what I like. You just buy whatever the stores put on the mannequins."

An idea pops into her head. I can tell because her eyes get huge and she sprints off with everyone's eyes following her. She leaps to the little kid play gym, only ten yards or so away, from when our school used to be the elementary school.

She jumps onto the roped bridge and reaches for the monkey bars. In a flash, she swings herself around and sits on top as half the crowd moves closer.

"I'm Cat Lady!" she says, lowering her voice and bugging out her eyes. She pushes her hands out like a jaguar on the prowl.

With laughter her fuel, she continues crawling over the bars and meowing.

"Enough!" I yell, and it echoes. "Listen, Horse Girl, you're the only one here who thinks you're the coolest."

Silence falls over the whole playground.

"Pff, I made Lame-o mad, everyone," Horse Girl says. But there's no instant laughter.

"You just float around, person to person, but you don't actually have a best friend at all, do you?" I wipe sweat from my forehead. "You know why? Because you're actually not nice at all. You're mean. I don't get why you make fun of my cat when you're OBSESSED with your horses. And you check yourself out in the mirror at every chance and you BRAG about everything. And that just makes people not really want to be your best friend."

I hope people don't notice that I'm shaking. My whole body is. I try to fold my arms at my chest, but that feels weird, so I put my right arm on my hip and lean to that side. I hope it makes me tougher, because inside, I know I'm a few seconds away from either passing out or running away at a full sprint.

Someone giggles behind me and says, "Oh, snap!"

"Paleeze, Easter. You're such a loser," Horse Girl says. But she's surprised, I can tell.

"Smell your own horse crap, Erica." Holy holy.

She leans back and stares at me for a few seconds. I try to swallow normally, but the desert conditions won't allow it, so I press my foot to the ground to cover the gulp sound.

"SHUT UP! Your mom is a hermit weirdo who—"

Before I can even react, there's a gasp from behind me. Wreni grabs my hand and tries to get me to follow her away.

"STOP, ERICA!" I shout.

Then she really crosses the line.

"I'm Mrs. Peters," she says, wobbling on her knees, holding an invisible glass and cigarette. "Go away people." She makes a shoo gesture with her hand.

I scan the crowd. People are uncomfortable, looking down and even walking away.

Wreni tugs on my sleeve and nods to walk away.

It's when I look back at Horse Girl up there, balancing on her knees, that I see the bees. At least three circling around her head!

Flipping noodles.

"Erica, don't move!" I'm stern.

She ignores and continues on, so I shout it again.

"BEEEES!"

While she is frozen up there, probably trying to decide if I am tricking or not, I climb up at ultra-speed and kneel at the top. I swing my lunch bag over her head, dragging two of the bees away from her head.

"AHH!" She climbs down backward and leaps to the grass at three or so feet from the bottom. She nearly knocks into Mrs. Ritz, who has finally moseyed on over to check out what the crowd is up to.

Erica is almost to the school doors by the time I reach the bottom and start running myself. Three bees are after me.

"Erica's seveeeeeerly allergic to beees," I shout as I pass Mrs. Ritz.

The bees call for backup, and in a jiffy, at least five trail me. I pretend to be an Olympic sprinter coming in for the finish. Hot tamales!

"Open. The. Door!" I shout to Connor who's standing next to it, looking shocked with his bottom lip hanging down.

When I get inside the school, I pull the heavy door closed, because Connor is moving in slow motion. Through the sliver of a window, I see the bees scatter.

I'm catching my breath when I hear the sniffling.

Erica's facing the hallway, crying.

"Did you," I ask, between deep breaths. "Get stung?"

"No," she whispers without turning "You?"

"I don't think so." I examine my legs and arms.

"I've never been stung, so I wouldn't know, anyway."

"You'd know."

"Oh, okay. Guess not then." I lean against the wall near her.

Silence lingers for a while.

"Your dad…" she says so sharply I nearly jump. "Fired my dad at Maggie Mae's like five or six years ago for something that wasn't even his fault. And since then, he hasn't been able to find an okay job."

"Oh." I'm so shocked, words are slow to hit my mouth. "I'm, I'm sorry."

"Yeah." Her mouth moves into a perfect frown.

"And why'd you turn Stephanie against me?"

"I didn't at all. I'm sorry that our friendship hurt you, though."

She nods and walks away to the bathroom.

I close my eyes for a second or two before the tapping on the door starts. Connor's face is pressed against it, looking very fish like and worried.

He is followed by Mrs. Ritz, who has come to check on Erica, and Wreni, who has come to check on me.

No one mentions the bee incident for the rest of the day and that is fine with me.

• • • THIRTY-TWO

With a good fifteen minutes still left in Science class, Mrs. Martin gives us our homework assignment and detention to a kid who groans and mumbles something about hating homework.

"Okay, now go ahead and use a few minutes to get started on the assignment," she instructs.

I'm refilling my mechanical pencil with lead when Mrs. Martin says, ultra upbeat, "Easter?"

"Yes?" I drop the sticks of lead and two roll off of my desk before I can catch them.

"I'd like you and Connor to please go make thirty copies of this handout," she says, smirking and waving a sheet of paper high in the air.

"Okay, sure." I nod. I feel sort of glad about hanging with Connor for a few minutes.

He's closer to the door, so I grab the sheet from

Mrs. Martin and meet him there. The door squeaks and clicks closed behind us.

"Look at that. I'm getting asked to do errands with Easter Peters. I must've made a good impression on Martin somehow," he says with full dimples. "That's gotta have a good effect on my progress report."

"That's right!" I laugh. "I take full credit for your academic achievements." This time, I punch his arm and he pretends it hurts by mouthing, "Yow!"

While we're standing at the copier outside of the principal's office, I don't even notice that none of the office people, not to mention the principal, are around. That is until I hear doors down the hall burst open and in a second, the hall is full of students headed toward the assembly room.

"What's going on?" I ask Connor.

"Hmm, I dunno." He shrugs like it's not totally weird and presses buttons on the copier so fast, the whole thing gets jammed up and beeps like a smoke detector.

"Brilliant!"

While I'm carefully pulling shreds of paper from the side of the machine, the principal's voice bellows through a static-y Public Announcement system. "Easter Peters, please come to the assembly room."

I shoot Connor an OMG look, but he nods like he knows what's up. "Let's go."

"What's going on?"

My legs are wobbly as we walk down the hallway.

I'm too nervous/shocked/panicked to speak. Connor opens the door and points his arm all gentleman-ly, like he's introducing a princess.

I meet hundreds of staring eyes. The entire Lake of Eileen Middle School student body and three rows of teachers are seated there, LIKE THEY'VE BEEN EXPECTING ME.

"Me?" I mouth to the principal after I step in.

"Wonderful. There she is," the principal says from the edge of the stage and shifts the microphone to his other hand. Connor puts his hand on my back and pushes me toward two empty seats in the front row and we sit. "Ladies and gentleman, we have a wonderful treat to share with you today. Music please, Mrs. Martin." The lights fade and the giant presentation screen rolls down.

"Photography by Easter Peters" appears in cursive-y, white typeface across a black screen. I let the folding chair slink me low. Familiar butterflies rush to my stomach like Yoplait to the sound of someone opening a yogurt cup.

Connor's watching for my reaction. I can feel his eyes on me, but my neck goes frozen so I can't turn.

Sparkly music hums between 'wows' and 'ooohs' as my photos of flowers, birds, the lake and shops on Main Street flash and fade on the screen.

When "The End" scrolls, all fancy across the screen, Wreni's voice rings out, "Yeeaaaah, yeah, Easter!" Then the whole room cheers and claps.

"Wow, awesome" and "good job" come from every direction. When I turn around, the first smile I catch is from Erica. And it's sort of, almost, genuine. I swear.

"Easter." The principal's voice echoes around the room. "We were so impressed with your photographic art that we submitted it to the Michigan State Department of Education. They have requested your work to be placed on display at the student section of the Michigan Museum of Contemporary Art, with your permission, of course."

"Sure, absolutely," I whisper, but I guess no one can hear me, because Connor nudges me and mouths, "louder." So, I stand and shout, "Yes, I'd be honored. Thank you."

At home, in Operation Cool, I write the whole story down and then, "I guess I already had a thing after all" with ten exclamation points and two smiley faces.

••• THIRTY-THREE

When you're twelve years old, teenagers are scary. Two years difference in age is really not a big deal when you're like eight and they're like ten but twelve and fourteen? That's a decade in the kid world. I'm a baby compared to them.

You can imagine my reaction when Grandma Dottie picks me up from school and says, "What our family is going through is extremely common. Pretty much everyone has a loved one who is battling alcoholism. The effects are devastating, especially on children."

I nod.

"There's a group of kids and teens who are going through the exact same thing as you. They get together every week to talk about it."

"Uhhh," I lean back in my seat.

"I think it'd be a great idea if you went. You can learn from them." She nods like she's believing it more and more as she speaks. "I think you'd really enjoy it and it'd be a great source of support for you."

"No way," I say confidently. "I'm not going to sit in a room full of strangers. Plus, I'm not a teenager, so..."

"You almost are," she says with patience, like a kindergarten teacher. "And there are others your age. They'd love to have you join. You can even just sit back and listen. You don't have to talk."

I shake my head and stare at the bumper of the car in front of us. "Mmm, thanks but I'd rather not."

"Well, how about you just go once, and if you don't like it, you don't ever have to go back."

It's really hard to argue with Grandma Dottie. She's too nice and I don't want to disappoint her.

"Okay, fine, but I don't have to talk, right? I can just listen?"

"Yes, absolutely."

On a Thursday night, butterflies are going crazy inside my belly when Grandma Dottie walks me inside of the church basement.

It's cold and dusty-attic smelly and I'm thinking that I might just pass out when I see a teenager with a beard pass us. A beard!

"Um, Grandma," I whisper as we near the meeting room door. "These teenagers are grownups." I might as well as be wearing a diaper.

This makes Grandma giggle, though I don't know why.

In the room, there are three tables pushed together and teenagers are laughing like they've known each other forever. There are colorful hand-made posters of trees, flowers, waterfalls and butterflies taped all over the walls.

Every kid's head looks up at me, and my knees lock, so I can't move from the doorway.

"Hi!" A girl who looks like she's sixteen with black hair, green eye shadow and a thick hot pink bracelet waves like she knows me, but I've never seen her before in my life.

A 'hi,' 'hey,' 'hello' and a nod or a wave follows from every one.

A kid who looks younger than me smiles.

"Come on in," someone says.

This gives me enough courage to step forward.

A guy with braces pulls a chair from a stack against the wall, unfolds it, and sets it up at the end of a table. "Have a seat," he says.

I glance back at Grandma Dottie and nod to let her know I'm okay and she can wait outside the door.

Grandma Dottie smiles back and leaves so I sit, still nervous and bouncing my leg.

A familiar voice says, "Easter!"

I spin to find Connor grinning the most ginormous smile I've ever seen.

"Connor?! What are you doing here?" I'm completely confused.

"I come here every week!" His smile grows taller, I swear, as he sets up a chair. The kid next to me makes room for him to squeeze in next to me.

In the doorway, another familiar face appears.

Erica.

She smiles when the room repeats the chorus of "hey, Erica," but she moves with only a tenth of the confidence she has at school.

In fact, if not for her ponytail, I might not even believe she's the same person.

She finds a seat directly across the table from me and sits.

Erica notices me, right away, and we stare for a few seconds.

Then she smiles.

Yep, SHE SMILES AT ME. In a nice way. Not a smirk.

I'm so surprised about Connor and Erica that I don't even notice when the green eye-shadow girl begins the meeting by reading from a paper all about why we're here—to support one another, to share our stories, to listen, to learn from one another, as we cope with the effects of a loved one's drinking addiction.

One by one, around the table, they each speak.

"My parents finally kicked my brother out of the house this week," Erica says softly to the middle of the table like she's fighting back a major cry. "He stole money from my mom's purse again and didn't come home for two days. Mom cried for hours. I hate how he hurts my mom and dad like this."

Just like that, I know her, the real her.

Stories about dads, moms, aunts, uncles, brothers, sisters, cousins and friends—they're all versions of the same story, through tears and laughter, about people they love drinking too much and doing hurtful things.

Then Connor clears his throat, glances at me and says, "Hi, I'm Connor."

"Hi, Connor," the room says together, but I forget to join because I'm so interested in what he's going to say.

"Well, my dad celebrated one year of sobriety this week," he says, scanning the room with a grin. The whole room claps, and I do, too. "Dad knew I'd wanted to see a film out last Friday so we all went, together. A few years ago, I went to the movies, by myself, to escape life at home." He adjusts his baseball cap and stares at the edge of the table. "My mother would never leave Dad at home, back then, when he was drinking. I'll never understand it but she just stayed there with him, worried the house would burn down or something. She was miserable—angry, nervous. I'm so glad that we're all able to enjoy life a lot more."

I decide not to speak, even though I feel I've known these people for years, not just minutes. When we all get up to leave when the hour's over, more than half the kids look directly at me when they say together, "Keep coming back."

Something about this room, being around people who've felt like I have, who've experienced things like me makes me feel better, makes me feel normal. I can't wait to come back.

• • • THIRTY-FOUR

Two weeks with no visiting nor talking on the phone with Mom makes things seem out of place, but it's been easy to get used to Grandma Dottie being around, taking care of things and always listening.

I'm thinking about Mom, though, a lot every day. I'm so mad at her sometimes. How could she let all of this happen? Why didn't she get help? Other times, I'm really sad because I miss her, I really do. And why does this have to be happening to my family? It's not fair! What if Mom gets worse, not better? What then?

When I start thinking too much, I read the books I got from the Alateen meeting and remember that I should take each day one at a time. I don't need to think so much about the past. I don't need to worry about the future. I'll make today the best possible.

But every night before I fall asleep, "what if"

245

haunt. Nothing guarantees that the treatment center will work. Even if she does get better, there's always the chance that she'll slip again and we'll end up right where we started all over again. I pray and pray for Mom. For Dad. For me.

At school, Mrs. Martin announces details about Friday's dance. Everyone should be creative in their outfits because it's 1970s themed. Wahoo! I get to bust out the vintage!

The day of the dance is exactly when Mom's treatment has passed the two-week mark, so she is allowed to have visitors and phone calls!

On Friday morning, Dad says, "I'll pick you up from school, then we'll go visit Mom for a while. Then we'll be back in time for the dance so you won't miss anything."

"Sounds good," I say. "Thanks."

Since all of the stuff happened, I've lost that fear of saying exactly what I'm wondering about, so without waiting, I ask Dad, "Are you nervous to see Mom?"

He's a little out of breath on account of having just carried in a new desk for Mom. He made a special place for it in the corner of their bedroom by the window so that she can write songs there, if she wants.

"I'd move it down a few more inches," I say motioning for him to scoot the desk down a bit. "There. Perfect!"

"Am I worried about Mom? Yes, I am. But she knows she has us so we just have to believe in her."

"Do you think she's okay there at the place?"

"I know she's okay and that she's doing better, but it's hard, Easter. Probably harder than we could ever imagine. It's a battle Mom will have to fight the rest of her life. But she has our support, and the only thing you should focus on is taking good care of yourself."

After school, it's a long drive to the treatment center, mostly because Dad and I are nervous and excited at the same time.

We are driving down a park-ish street with lots of trees lining on both sides. It is more city-like than country and Mom probably likes that.

"Here it is." Dad points to a long brick building with a circle driveway and rows and rows of trees with pearly stringed lights.

"It's nice!" I roll down the window for a closer look at the landscaping. "Looks like a hotel."

Mom's waiting on a bench in the lobby when we come through the front door. She looks so pretty and definitely healthier minus the puffy, red eyes. She is wearing the blue sweater I gave her for Christmas and her hair is smooth and shiny in a low ponytail.

But it isn't until she smiles that I really recognize Mom, the old version of her, I mean. Her eyes have some sparkle again, as corny as that may sound.

We hug for a long time before I let go so she can

greet Dad. It is the first time in forever that I've seen them kiss.

"Let me show you around," she says, pointing down a long hallway with dozens of doors.

It smells like a hospital and a wedding mixed together on account of pine tree-ish cleaning and a crazy amount of flowers.

Mom opens the door to her room and we follow inside. There are two beds, two desks and a dresser. The beds are perfectly made and there isn't a speck of dust to be found.

"It's so clean!"

I think Mom likes that compliment because she nods and smiles.

"There was another woman staying here, too, in this room but yesterday, she checked herself out. She told everyone that she could handle her problem on her own. It was really sad because the staff here said she's already been here twice before. But she doesn't have a wonderful, supportive family like I do."

Mom sits down on the bed and pats the spot beside her for me to sit.

"I do feel better already," she whispers close to my face. "There's a long, long road ahead of me but I know I'm on the right track."

Dad rubs Mom's shoulder.

"Enough about me! How are you? How's school?"

After I give the full report, she whispers, "That's my girl" while hugging me tight.

Dad picks up a framed photo from Mom's desk.

"This is my all-time favorite," Dad announces, holding it out for me to see.

It's a shot of three of us laughing hysterically about who knows what at a family picnic.

As she walks us out, Mom tells us her daily schedule: breakfast, exercise, meetings with a group of people with the same problems who gather together to give each other support and share their stories and experiences, lunch and then one-on-one meetings with her counselor, dinner and some kind of activity like movie watching.

The most valuable part of the whole thing, Mom says, is her sponsor. She's a lady who drank away twenty years of her life, but she successfully gave it up and hasn't had a drink for twelve years. Now she volunteers her time to help other people battle it, too.

"I can call her at any time when I'm having a rough time," she says. I am glad Mom has someone who can relate to her illness better than us.

Before we leave, Mom smoothes out my hair with a hairdryer and big round brush. It's frizz free for the dance!

I hug Mom for a really long time. She says, "I love you more than can be expressed with words. No matter what, always know that, okay?"

"Okay."

My ballet flats squeak against the tile floor. Dad and I pile into his truck and Mom waves as we drive away.

I cry right away, once out of Mom's sight.

"Easter?!" Dad's totally confused.

I stare out the window because I don't know how to explain why I'm upset. Finally, I say, "I'm just so worried that now things will go back to being really bad."

"Oh, honey," Dad says. "That's understandable, given everything that you've been through. It's still going to be a long, tough road to recovery for Mom and for us. That's for sure. But the good news is that we're going to get through it together. You opened my eyes to the severity of the situation and it will never, ever go back to how it was."

I press my head against the glass without responding.

"Easter?"

"Yes, thanks, Dad."

I believe him with all my heart, I really do.

• • • THIRTY-FIVE

Wreni waits for me at the front door of the school and waves when Dad's truck squeaks to a stop and I jump out.

Dad smiles and says, "Have a good time tonight."

Inside, Wreni and I don't waste any time. We follow the music and get right into the crowd of seventh graders and eighth graders. I move my hips to the left and to the right and throw my hands in the air and jam on invisible drums high above my head.

"See, you have rhythm, girl," Wreni spins around and claps at just the right parts of the song.

Wreni makes up some kind of crazy robot dance and we die laughing.

The punch/cookie table catches my eye. Connor is staring at me. We wave at the same time, but he stays by the table.

I have a serious case of desert tongue, so I head to the hallway door and my platform shoes slide across the tile floor. I gather my hair and lean into the drinking fountain and hydrate like Amigo does on a hot summer day.

"You make a sweet seventies girl," Connor says from behind me.

I have a mouthful like a blowfish when I turn my head, so I swallow fast and a drop of water rolls down my chin.

Inside my stomach, butterflies groove to the beat of the music. This time, I'm glad they're there.

Get a grip, Easter. It's just Connor.

"You have some dancin' skills," he says and rocks back on his feet.

"Ha, well, I have to make up for my Talent Show screw up," I say, smiling and exhaling super loudly, like I just finished a marathon or something. I wipe my forehead and not-so-smoothly dry my hand on the side of my leg.

Silence echoes.

"Seriously, I think you even wowed Mrs. Martin," he says. "I saw her tapping her orthopedic shoes and bobbing her head. Don't be surprised if she asks for Miss Easter Ann Peters Dance Lessons." I like the way he says it like a game show host, all official. His dimples appear.

"Thanks." My legs turn Jell-O-y. I'm cold and hot the same time and nervous in a way that I don't want to fade.

The music ramps up again, so with a burst of guts and without really thinking, I say "Let's dance!" and grab Connor's hand and pull him behind me, through the doors and to the center of the gym.

"Okay, sweet!"

We dance. He holds my hand and spins me around a few times. It's as fun as a carnival Tilt-A-Whirl and familiar like we've danced a thousand times before.

"I could dance with you until the cows come home," he says real loud over the music as I shimmy away a few feet and spin back near him.

"Movie quote?" This time I don't look at him like he's nuts.

"Yup. 1933. Groucho Marx. Duck Soup."

"Kay, thanks, Movie Encyclopedia."

"Welcome," he says as the music gets faster.

Wreni sways on over and the three of us make up funny moves. Picture a disco queen, a sprinkler and a fish breaking it down. My muscles burn but I can't stop laughing, even if I try.

That night, I write "success" all huge in my Operation Cool notebook with purple and hot pink markers and add three exclamation points for effect.

Yoplait leaps onto my bed and takes two minutes to find the comfiest part before curling up and wrapping herself with her tail.

I slip Operation Cool into my nightstand drawer,

turn the warm knob on my bedside lamp and slide under my covers.

"Life is always going to be twistier and turnier than you want it to be," I whisper to Yoplait. She blinks twice, like 'That's great, but I'm going to sleep now.'

"You just have to take good care of yourself. Do that and everything will fall into place. That's all. Isn't that cool?"

ABOUT THE AUTHOR

© Michael Shuster Photography

Jody Lamb writes stories for the young in age and at heart. Luckily, she's pretty much the same person she was at twelve years old, even though she's a grownup now. Jody loves books, writing, ugly dogs, peppermint ice cream, ear-to-ear smiles, insides-twisting laughter and her family. She is a passionate advocate for kids with alcoholic loved ones. Like Easter Ann, Jody lives in Michigan with furry friends. She hopes you'll say hello at www.JodyLamb.com.

ACKNOWLEDGMENTS

You rock, really.

If I were standing next to you at this very moment, I'd give you a high five and a hug. You see, you're the reason I wrote this story and, therefore, you are worthy of acknowledgement! Thank you for reading.

You've joined the ranks of these remarkable people:

My extraordinary sister, Brooke Lamb, read every word of every draft of this book and told me when it stunk (with a scrunched-up face), sounded too grownup-ish (with a get-real face) and when it was actually quite good (smiles and laughter). When I almost gave up hope that this would ever be a book to share with you, she convinced me I had no choice but to push on. Brooke, you are forever my guardian angel. I am grateful for your inspiration, contagious love of life and old-lady wisdom. I love you! Keep shooting for the moon and coloring the sky while you're at.

Mom? Thank you for planting compassion seeds in

me very early on. I admire your heart. Dad? Thank you for teaching me the importance of determination and bravery by your example and for your constant support. I love you both.

My giant, crazy family cheered me on from the beginning, especially my hilarious and brilliant cousins Maria and Alexis Demos. Thank you! Jillian Evelyn, my sweet cousin like a sista, your talent blows my mind. Thank you for graciously accepting the assignment to create the art for this novel. (Isn't she incredibly talented? I know!) You brought Easter and Yoplait to life and tears to my eyes.

When I was a kid, a few people gave me dusty old books and with enthusiasm, told me to write my own some day. My amazing grandmothers and my late Grandpa Bill Lamb? With thanks, here's the first of many.

You know who's sweet? Writers! Countless accomplished and aspiring authors were generous in advice and you-can-do-it conversations. At the top of that tall list is Jane Ratcliffe, my instructor in a creative writing class, who read the beginning of this story three years ago and said, "Keep going. You really must keep going." Jane, if not for your belief in me, this story would be a forgotten homework assignment.

Sarah Perry, my dearest author friend, kindly took a seat beside me on the writing rollercoaster and shared helpings of encouragement and laughter, just when I needed it most. Double high five to you, Sarah.

Ultra-talented author Karen Day, you? Thank you

for your kindness, especially when I was a publishing world newbie.

Thank you to Kim Hytinen, Rachael Perry, Darci Hannah and all of the South Lyon Writers for reading drafts of this story, channeling their inner twelve-year-old, patting me on the back and politely kicking me in the butt when it was ready to be shared with the world.

The rest of you marvelous writers know who you are!

Thank you, courageous Jennifer Baum of Scribe Publishing, for taking a chance on a debut author and for believing in the story, Easter Ann, the subject and me.

The inspirational, tireless Jerry Moe, Vice President and Director of the Children's Program at Betty Ford Center, gave me an amazing gift. Let me tell you, a high-five call about this book from Jerry Moe is like a call from your favorite athletes and rock bands all at once, for me. Jerry? Thank you for your kindness and encouragement. You're a superstar.

A gazillion years ago, my best friends Mary Casey Cretu, Erin Gendernalik Brown and Keith and Katie Woods heard of my writing dreams. Make it happen, they urged often. Thank you, guys. And, Grace, my smiley goddaughter? Thank you for making up stories with me. Love you!

People I've met on elevators, on airplanes, at Al-Anon meetings, in the blogging world and while standing in line for ice cream, heads up! Your thoughts about life and well wishes mean so much to me. You know who you are.

I'm forever grateful to my furry friends, like Easter's Amigo and Yoplait, who've left paw prints on my soul and were heroes during the toughest parts of my life.

And finally, to young people coping with loved ones' alcoholism and other addictions: you are in my heart, in my thoughts, in my prayers and you fuel my hope each and every day. You are the strongest, kindest people around and you inspire me. Hold tightly to hope and your dreams, and let them lead you, ya hear?

High five, hugs and kisses.

Please say hello and keep in touch. I'd like that very much! My contact info is at www.JodyLamb.com.

-Jody

RESOURCES
...for young people worried about or negatively affected by a loved one's drinking

You are not alone. Researchers estimate that 10 to 25 percent of children in the United States live with at least one parent who abuses alcohol. That means as many as one in four of your classmates are going through the same stuff as you.

Alateen
www.al-anon.alateen.org; wso@al-anon.org
Find a meeting near you by calling 1-888-4AL-ANON (1-888-425-2666) Monday-Friday, 8 am to 6 pm ET.

Alateen groups meet in community centers, churches, schools or other suitable places. It's a safe place to go every week to relax and be yourself among friends who have alcoholic loved ones, too. There you can let your guard down, share about what's happening in your life or just listen.

"Alateen is a mutual support group program for teenagers affected by a relative or friend's drinking. Some groups will accept members between the ages of 10 to 12. It is part of the Al-Anon Family Groups®

organization for family and friends of alcoholics. Alateen groups meet in the U.S., Canada, Puerto Rico, Bermuda, and worldwide. Although a separate entity, the Al-Anon/Alateen program is adapted from the Twelve Steps of Alcoholics Anonymous. Alateen members exchange their personal applications of the Al-Anon/Alateen program to their lives with each other without giving each other advice. Alateen meetings are facilitated by its members. However, adult Alateen Group Sponsors, who are experienced Al-Anon members, are present in an advisory and volunteer capacity. Whether or not the drinker is living or deceased, the only requirement for Alateen membership is for teens to have been or currently be concerned about another person's drinking. There are no dues or fees for membership. No appointment or referral is necessary."

– From Al-Anon Family Group Headquarters

ChildHelp USA Child Abuse Hotline: 1-800-422-4453. If you do not feel safe, please call this number and a counselor will help you.

"ChildHelp USA is dedicated to the prevention of child abuse. Serving the United States, its territories, and Canada, the Hotline is staffed 24 hours a day, 7 days a week with professional crisis counselors who, through interpreters, can provide assistance in 170 languages. The Hotline offers crisis intervention, information, literature, and referrals to thousands of emergency, social service, and support resources. All calls are anonymous and confidential."

– From ChildHelp USA

Facts about alcoholism on the web

National Association for Children of Alcoholics: www.nacoa.org/kidspage.html

In the UK: www.nacoa.org.uk • UK Helpline: 0800 358 3456

Children of Alcoholics Foundation: www.coaf.org

National Institute on Alcohol Abuse and Alcoholism: www.niaaa.nih.gov

Books

Al-Anon Family Group Headquarters, Inc. *Courage to Be Me—Living with Alcoholism*. Virginia, 1996. This book is a collection of writings and drawings by Alateen members who have been affected by another person's drinking.

Al-Anon Family Group Headquarters, Inc. *Alateen—a day at a time*. Virginia, 1983. This book shares a dose of inspiration written by Alateen members for every year of the year.

The most important resource of all

YOU! Your only responsibility in life is to take good care of yourself. If you do not feel safe, please tell a grownup you trust and reach out for help. You deserve safety and serenity.